WITHDRAWN

Just Folks

By

Edgar A. Guest

Lightyear Press
Laurel New York

International Standard Book Number: 0-89968-241-3

For ordering information, contact:

Lightyear Press
P.O. Box 507
Laurel, New York 11948

To the Little Mother
and the Memory of the Big Father,
This Simple Book
Is Affectionately Dedicated

INDEX

Index

Index

Index

Just Folks

Just Folks

We're queer folks here.
  We'll talk about the weather,
  The good times we have had together,
The good times near,
    The roses buddin', an' the bees
    Once more upon their nectar sprees;
    The scarlet fever scare, an' who
    Came mighty near not pullin' through,
    An' who had light attacks, an' all
    The things that int'rest, big or small;
But here you'll never hear of sinnin'
Or any scandal that's beginnin'.
We've got too many other labors
To scatter tales that harm our neighbors.

We're strange folks here.
  We're tryin' to be cheerful,
  An' keep this home from gettin' tearful.
We hold it dear;
    Too dear for pettiness an' meanness,
    An' nasty tales of men's uncleanness.
    Here you shall come to joyous smilin',
    Secure from hate an' harsh revilin';
    Here, where the wood fire brightiy blazes,
    You'll hear from us our neighbor's praises.

Here, that they'll never grow to doubt us,
We keep our friends always about us;
An' here, though storms outside may pelter
Is refuge for our friends, an' shelter.

We've one rule here,
    An' that is to be pleasant.
    The folks we know are always present,
Or very near.
    An' though they dwell in many places,
    We think we're talkin' to their faces;
    An' that keeps us from only seein'
    The faults in any human bein',
    An' checks our tongues when they'd go trailin'
    Into the mire of mortal failin'.
Flaws aren't so big when folks are near you;
You don't talk mean when they can hear you.
An' so no scandal here is started,
Because from friends we're never parted.

As It Goes

In the corner she's left the mechanical toy,
    On the chair is her Teddy Bear fine;
The things that I thought she would really enjoy
    Don't seem to be quite in her line.

12

There's the flaxen-haired doll that is lovely to see
  And really expensively dressed,
Left alone, all uncared for, and strange though
    it be,
  She likes her rag dolly the best.

Oh, the money we spent and the plans that we
    laid
  And the wonderful things that we bought!
There are toys that are cunningly, skillfully
    made,
  But she seems not to give them a thought.
She was pleased when she woke and discovered
    them there,
  But never a one of us guessed
That it isn't the splendor that makes a gift
    rare—
  She likes her rag dolly the best.

There's the flaxen-haired doll, with the real
    human hair,
  There's the Teddy Bear left all alone,
There's the automobile at the foot of the stair,
  And there is her toy telephone;
We thought they were fine, but a little child's
    eyes
  Look deeper than ours to find charm,
And now she's in bed, and the rag dolly lies
  Snuggled close on her little white arm.

Hollyhocks

Old-fashioned flowers! I love them all:
The morning-glories on the wall,
The pansies in their patch of shade,
The violets, stolen from a glade,
The bleeding hearts and columbine,
Have long been garden friends of mine;
But memory every summer flocks
About a clump of hollyhocks.

The mother loved them years ago;
Beside the fence they used to grow,
And though the garden changed each year
And certain blooms would disappear
To give their places in the ground
To something new that mother found,
Some pretty bloom or rosebush rare—
The hollyhocks were always there.

It seems but yesterday to me
She led me down the yard to see
The first tall spires, with bloom aflame,
And taught me to pronounce their name.
And year by year I watched them grow,
The first flowers I had come to know.
And with the mother dear I'd yearn
To see the hollyhocks return.

The garden of my boyhood days
With hollyhocks was kept ablaze;
In all my recollections they
In friendly columns nod and sway;
And when to-day their blooms I see,
Always the mother smiles at me;
The mind's bright chambers, life unlocks
Each summer with the hollyhocks.

Sacrifice

When he has more than he can eat
To feed a stranger's not a feat.

When he has more than he can spend
It isn't hard to give or lend.

Who gives but what he'll never miss
Will never know what giving is.

He'll win few praises from his Lord
Who does but what he can afford.

The widow's mite to heaven went
Because real sacrifice it meant.

Reward

Don't want medals on my breast,
   Don't want all the glory,
I'm not worrying greatly lest
   The world won't hear my story.
A chance to dream beside a stream
   Where fish are biting free;
A day or two, 'neath skies of blue,
   Is joy enough for me.

I do not ask a hoard of gold,
   Nor treasures rich and rare;
I don't want all the joys to hold;
   I only want a share.
Just now and then, away from men
   And all their haunts of pride,
If I can steal, with rod and reel,
   I will be satisfied.

I'll gladly work my way through life;
   I would not always play;
I only ask to quit the strife
   For an occasional day.
If I can sneak from toil a week
   To chum with stream and tree,
I'll fish away and smiling say
   That life's been good to me.

See It Through

When you're up against a trouble,
  Meet it squarely, face to face;
Lift your chin and set your shoulders,
  Plant your feet and take a brace.
When it's vain to try to dodge it,
  Do the best that you can do;
You may fail, but you may conquer,
  See it through!

Black may be the clouds about you
  And your future may seem grim,
But don't let your nerve desert you;
  Keep yourself in fighting trim.
If the worst is bound to happen,
  Spite of all that you can do,
Running from it will not save you,
  See it through!

Even hope may seem but futile,
  When with troubles you're beset,
But remember you are facing
  Just what other men have met.
You may fail, but fall still fighting;
  Don't give up, whate'er you do;
Eyes front, head high to the finish.
  See it through!

To the Humble

If all the flowers were roses,
  If never daisies grew,
If no old-fashioned posies
  Drank in the morning dew,
Then man might have some reason
  To whimper and complain,
And speak these words of treason,
  That all our toil is vain.

If all the stars were Saturns
  That twinkle in the night,
Of equal size and patterns,
  And equally as bright,
Then men in humble places,
  With humble work to do,
With frowns upon their faces
  Might trudge their journey through.

But humble stars and posies
  Still do their best, although
They're planets not, nor roses,
  To cheer the world below.
And those old-fashioned daisies
  Delight the soul of man;
They're here, and this their praise is:
  They work the Master's plan.

Though humble be your labor,
　And modest be your sphere,
Come, envy not your neighbor
　Whose light shines brighter **here.**
Does God forget the daisies
　Because the roses bloom?
Shall you not win His praises
　By toiling at your loom?

Have you, the toiler humble,
　Just reason to complain,
To shirk your task and grumble
　And think that it is vain
Because you see a brother
　With greater work to do?
No fame of his can smother
　The merit that's in you.

When Nellie's on the Job

The bright spots in my life are when the servant
    quits the place,
Although that grim disturbance brings a frown
    to Nellie's face;
The week between the old girl's reign and entry
    of the new
Is one that's filled with happiness and comfort
    through and through.
The charm of living's back again—a charm that
    servants rob—
I like the home, I like the meals, when Nellie's
    on the job.

There's something in a servant's ways, however
    fine they be,
That has a cold and distant touch and frets the
    soul of me.
The old home never looks so well, as in that
    week or two
That we are servantless and Nell has all the
    work to do.
There is a sense of comfort then that makes my
    pulses throb
And home is as it ought to be when Nellie's on
    the job.

Think not that I'd deny her help or grudge the
    servant's pay;
When one departs we try to get another right
    away;
I merely state the simple fact that no such joys
    I've known
As in those few brief days at home when we've
    been left alone.
There is a gentleness that seems to soothe this
    selfish elf
And, Oh, I like to eat those meals that Nellie
    gets herself!

You cannot buy the gentle touch that mother
    gives the place;
No servant girl can do the work with just the
    proper grace.
And though you hired the queen of cooks to
    fashion your croquettes,
Her meals would not compare with those your
    loving comrade gets;
So, though the maid has quit again, and she is
    moved to sob,
The old home's at its finest now, for Nellie's
    on the job.

The Old, Old Story

I have no wish to rail at fate,
   And vow that I'm unfairly treated;
I do not give vent to my hate
   Because at times I am defeated.
Life has its ups and downs, I know,
   But tell me why should people say
Whenever after fish I go:
   "You should have been here yesterday"?

It is my luck always to strike
   A day when there is nothing doing,
When neither perch, nor bass, nor pike
   My baited hooks will come a-wooing.
Must I a day late always be?
   When not a nibble comes my way
Must someone always say to me:
   "We caught a bunch here yesterday"?

I am not prone to discontent,
   Nor over-zealous now to climb;
If victory is not yet meant
   For me I'll calmly bide my time.
But I should like just once to go
   Out fishing on some lake or bay
And not have someone mutter: "Oh,
   You should have been here yesterday."

The Pup

He tore the curtains yesterday,
  And scratched the paper on the wall;
Ma's rubbers, too, have gone astray—
  She says she left them in the hall;
He tugged the table cloth and broke
  A fancy saucer and a cup;
Though Bud and I think it a joke
  Ma scolds a lot about the pup.

The sofa pillows are a sight,
  The rugs are looking somewhat frayed,
And there is ruin, left and right,
  That little Boston bull has made.
He slept on Buddy's counterpane—
  Ma found him there when she woke up.
I think it needless to explain
  She scolds a lot about the pup.

And yet he comes and licks her hand
  And sometimes climbs into her lap
And there, Bud lets me understand,
  He very often takes his nap.
And Bud and I have learned to know
  She wouldn't give the rascal up:
She's really fond of him, although
  She scolds a lot about the pup.

Since Jessie Died

We understand a lot of things we never did
    before,
And it seems that to each other Ma and I are
    meaning more.
I don't know how to say it, but since little Jessie
    died
We have learned that to be happy we must travel
    side by side.
You can share your joys and pleasures, but you
    never come to know
The depth there is in loving, till you've got a
    common woe.

We're past the hurt of fretting—we can talk
    about it now:
She slipped away so gently and the fever left
    her brow
So softly that we didn't know we'd lost her, but,
    instead,
We thought her only sleeping as we watched
    beside her bed.
Then the doctor, I remember, raised his head, as
    if to say
What his eyes had told already, and Ma fainted
    dead away.

Up to then I thought that money was the thing
   I ought to get;
And I fancied, once I had it, I should never have
   to fret.
But I saw that I had wasted precious hours in
   seeking wealth;
I had made a tidy fortune, but I couldn't buy
   her health.
And I saw this truth much clearer than I'd ever
   seen before:
That the rich man and the poor man have to let
   death through the door.

We're not half so keen for money as one time
   we used to be;
I am thinking more of mother and she's thinking more of me.
Now we spend more time together, and I know
   we're meaning more
To each other on life's journey, than we ever
   meant before.
It was hard to understand it! Oh, the dreary
   nights we've cried!
But we've found the depth of loving, since the
   day that Jessie died.

Hard Luck

Ain't no use as I can see
In sittin' underneath a tree
An' growlin' that your luck is bad,
An' that your life is extry sad;
Your life ain't sadder than your neighbor's
Nor any harder are your labors;
It rains on him the same as you,
An' he has work he hates to do;
An' he gits tired an'.he gits cross,
An' he has trouble with the boss;
You take his whole life, through an' through,
Why, he's no better off than you.

If whinin' brushed the clouds away
I wouldn't have a word to say;
If it made good friends out o' foes
I'd whine a bit, too, I suppose;
But when I look around an' see
A lot o' men resemblin' me,
An' see 'em sad, an' see 'em gay
With work t' do most every day,
Some full o' fun, some bent with care,
Some havin' troubles hard to bear,
I reckon, as I count my woes,
They're 'bout what everybody knows.

The day I find a man who'll say
He's never known a rainy day,

Who'll raise his right hand up an' swear
In forty years he's had no care,
Has never had a single blow,
An' never known one touch o' woe,
Has never seen a loved one die,
Has never wept or heaved a sigh,
Has never had a plan go wrong,
But allus laughed his way along;
Then I'll sit down an' start to whine
That all the hard luck here is mine.

Vacation Time

Vacation time! How glad it seemed
When as a boy I sat and dreamed
Above my school books, of the fun
That I should claim when toil was done;
And, Oh, how oft my youthful eye
Went wandering with the patch of sky
That drifted by the window panes
O'er pleasant fields and dusty lanes,
Where I would race and romp and shout
The very moment school was out.
My artful little fingers then
Feigned labor with the ink and pen,
But heart and mind were far away,
Engaged in some glad bit of play.

The last two weeks dragged slowly by;
Time hadn't then learned how to fly.
It seemed the clock upon the wall
From hour to hour could only crawl,
And when the teacher called my name,
Unto my cheeks the crimson came,
For I could give no answer clear
To questions that I didn't hear.
"Wool gathering, were you?" oft she said
And smiled to see me blushing red.
Her voice had roused me from a dream
Where I was fishing in a stream,
And, if I now recall it right,
Just at the time I had a bite.

And now my youngsters dream of play
In just the very selfsame way;
And they complain that time is slow
And that the term will never go.
Their little minds with plans are filled
For joyous hours they soon will build,
And it is vain for me to say,
That have grown old and wise and gray,
That time is swift, and joy is brief;
They'll put no faith in such belief.
To youthful hearts that long for play
Time is a laggard on the way.
'Twas, Oh, so slow to me back then
Ere I had learned the ways of men!

The Little Hurts

Every night she runs to me
With a bandaged arm or a bandaged knee,
A stone-bruised heel or a swollen brow,
And in sorrowful tones she tells me how
She fell and "hurted herse'f to-day"
While she was having the "bestest play."

And I take her up in my arms and kiss
The new little wounds and whisper this:
"Oh, you must be careful, my little one,
You mustn't get hurt while your daddy's gone,
For every cut with its ache and smart
Leaves another bruise on your daddy's heart."

Every night I must stoop to see
The fresh little cuts on her arm or knee;
The little hurts that have marred her play,
And brought the tears on a happy day;
For the path of childhood is oft beset
With care and trouble and things that fret.

Oh, little girl, when you older grow,
Far greater hurts than these you'll know;
Greater bruises will bring your tears,
Around the bend of the lane of years,
But come to your daddy with them at night
And he'll do his best to make all things right.

The Lanes of Memory

Adown the lanes of memory bloom all the
   flowers of yesteryear,
And looking back we smile to see life's bright
   red roses reappear,
The little sprigs of mignonette that smiled upon
   us as we passed,
The pansy and the violet, too sweet, we thought
   those days, to last.

The gentle mother by the door caresses still her
   lilac blooms,
And as we wander back once more we seem to
   smell the old perfumes,
We seem to live again the joys that once were
   ours so long ago
When we were little girls and boys, with all the
   charms we used to know.

But living things grow old and fade; the dead
   in memory remain,
In all their splendid youth arrayed, exempt from
   suffering and pain;
The little babe God called away, so many, many
   years ago,
Is still a little babe to-day, and I am glad that
   this is so.

Time has not changed the joys we knew; the
    summer rains or winter snows
Have failed to harm the wondrous hue of any
    dew-kissed bygone rose;
In memory 'tis still as fair as when we plucked
    it for our own,
And we can see it blooming there, if anything,
    more lovely grown.

Adown the lanes of memory bloom all the joys
    of yesteryear,
And God has given you and me the power to
    make them reappear;
For we can settle back at night and live again
    the joys we knew
And taste once more the old delight of days
    when all our skies were blue.

The Day of Days

A year is filled with glad events:
    The best is Christmas day,
But every holiday presents
    Its special round of play,
And looking back on boyhood now
    And all the charms it knew,
One day, above the rest, somehow,
    Seems brightest in review.

31

That day was finest, I believe,
  Though many grown-ups scoff,
When mother said that we could leave
  Our shoes and stockings off.

Through all the pleasant days of spring
  We begged to know once more
The joy of barefoot wandering
  And quit the shoes we wore;
But always mother shook her head
  And answered with a smile:
"It is too soon, too soon," she said.
  "Wait just a little while."
Then came that glorious day at last
  When mother let us know
That fear of taking cold was past
  And we could barefoot go.

Though Christmas day meant much to me,
  And eagerly I'd try
The first boy on the street to be
  The Fourth day of July,
I think the summit of my joy
  Was reached that happy day
Each year, when, as a barefoot boy,
  I hastened out to play.
Could I return to childhood fair,
  That day I think I'd choose
When mother said I needn't wear
  My stockings and my shoes.

A Fine Sight

I reckon the finest sight of all
   That a man can see in this world of ours
Ain't the works of art on the gallery wall,
   Or the red an' white o' the fust spring flowers,
Or a hoard o' gold from the yellow mines;
   But the sight that'll make ye want t' yell
Is t' catch a glimpse o' the fust pink signs
   In yer baby's cheek, that she's gittin well.

When ye see the pink jes' a-creepin' back
   T' the pale, drawn cheek, an' ye note a smile,
Then th' cords o' yer heart that were tight, grow
     slack
   An' ye jump fer joy every little while,
An' ye tiptoe back to her little bed
   As though ye doubted yer eyes, or were
Afraid it was fever come back instead,
   An' ye found that th' pink still blossomed there.

Ye've watched fer that smile an' that bit o' bloom
   With a heavy heart fer weeks an' weeks;
An' a castle o' joy becomes that room
   When ye glimpse th' pink in yer baby's cheeks.
An' out o' yer breast flies a weight o' care,
   An' ye're lifted up by some magic spell,
An' yer heart jes' naturally beats a prayer
   O' joy to the Lord 'cause she's gittin' well.

33

Manhood's Greeting

I've felt some little thrills of pride, I've inwardly
    rejoiced
Along the pleasant lanes of life to hear my
    praises voiced;
No great distinction have I claimed, but in a
    humble way
Some satisfactions sweet have come to brighten
    many a day;
But of the joyous thrills of life the finest that
    could be
Was mine upon that day when first a stranger
    "mistered" me.

I had my first long trousers on, and wore a
    derby too,
But I was still a little boy to everyone I knew.
I dressed in manly fashion, and I tried to act
    the part,
But I felt that I was awkward and lacked the
    manly art.
And then that kindly stranger spoke my name
    and set me free;
I was sure I'd come to manhood on the day he
    "mistered" me.

I never shall forget the joy that suddenly was
   mine,
The sweetness of the thrill that seemed to dance
   along my spine,
The pride that swelled within me, as he shook
   my youthful hand
And treated me as big enough with grown up
   men to stand.
I felt my body straighten and a stiffening at each
   knee,
And was gloriously happy, just because he'd
   "mistered" me.

I cannot now recall his name, I only wish I
   could.
I've often wondered if that day he really under-
   stood
How much it meant unto a boy, still wearing
   boyhood's tan,
To find that others noticed that he'd grown to
   be a man.
Now I try to treat as equal every growing boy
   I see
In memory of that kindly man—the first to
   "mister" me.

Fishing Nooks

"Men will grow weary," said the Lord,
"Of working for their bed and board.
They'll weary of the money chase
And want to find a resting place
Where hum of wheel is never heard
And no one speaks an angry word,
And selfishness and greed and pride
And petty motives don't abide.
They'll need a place where they can go
To wash their souls as white as snow.
They will be better men and true
If they can play a·day or two."

The Lord then made the brooks to flow
And fashioned rivers here below,
And many lakes; for water seems
Best suited for a mortal's dreams.
He placed about them willow trees
To catch the murmur of the breeze,
And sent the birds that sing the best
Among the foliage to nest.
He filled each pond and stream and lake
With fish for man to come and take;
Then stretched a velvet carpet deep
On which a weary soul could sleep.

It seemed to me the Good Lord knew
That man would want something to do

When worn and wearied with the stress
Of battling hard for world success.
When sick at heart of all the strife
And pettiness of daily life,
He knew he'd need, from time to time,
To cleanse himself of city grime,
And he would want some place to be
Where hate and greed he'd never see.
And so on lakes and streams and brooks
The Good Lord fashioned fishing nooks.

Show the Flag

Show the flag and let it wave
As a symbol of the brave;
Let it float upon the breeze
As a sign for each who sees
That beneath it, where it rides,
Loyalty to-day abides.

Show the flag and signify
That it wasn't born to die;
Let its colors speak for you
That you still are standing true,
True in sight of God and man
To the work that flag began.

Show the flag that all may see
That you serve humanity.
Let it whisper to the breeze
That comes singing through the trees
That whatever storms descend
You'll be faithful to the end.

Show the flag and let it fly,
Cheering every passer-by.
Men that may have stepped aside,
May have lost their old-time pride,
May behold it there, and then,
Consecrate themselves again.

Show the flag! The day is gone
When men blindly hurry on
Serving only gods of gold;
Now the spirit that was cold
Warms again to courage fine.
Show the flag and fall in line!

Constant Beauty

It's good to have the trees again, the singing of
the breeze again,
It's good to see the lilacs bloom as lovely as
of old.
It's good that we can feel again the touch of
beauties real again,

For hearts and minds, of sorrow now, have
all that they can hold.

The roses haven't changed a bit, nor have the
lilacs stranged a bit,
They bud and bloom the way they did before
the war began.
The world is upside down to-day, there's much
to make us frown to-day,
And gloom and sadness everywhere beset the
path of man.

But now the lilacs bloom again and give us their
perfume again,
And now the roses smile at us and nod along
the way;
And it is good to see again the blossoms on each
tree again,
And feel that nature hasn't changed the way
we have to-day.

Oh, we have changed from what we were; we're
not the carefree lot we were;
Our hearts are filled with sorrow now and
grave concern and pain,
But it is good to see once more, the blooming
lilac tree once more,
And find the constant roses here to comfort
us again.

A Patriotic Creed

To serve my country day by day
At any humble post I may;
To honor and respect her flag,
To live the traits of which I brag;
To be American in deed
As well as in my printed creed.

To stand for truth and honest toil,
To till my little patch of soil,
And keep in mind the debt I owe
To them who died that I might know
My country, prosperous and free,
And passed this heritage to me.

I always must in trouble's hour
Be guided by the men in power;
For God and country I must live,
My best for God and country give;
No act of mine that men may scan
Must shame the name American.

To do my best and play my part,
American in mind and heart;
To serve the flag and bravely stand
To guard the glory of my land;
To be American in deed:
God grant me strength to keep this creed!

Home

The road to laughter beckons me,
  The road to all that's best;
The home road where I nightly see
  The castle of my rest;
The path where all is fine and fair,
  And little children run,
For love and joy are waiting there
  As soon as day is done.

There is no rich reward of fame
  That can compare with this:
At home I wear an honest name,
  My lips are fit to kiss.
At home I'm always brave and strong,
  And with the setting sun
They find no trace of shame or wrong
  In anything I've done.

There shine the eyes that only see
  The good I've tried to do;
They think me what I'd like to be;
  They know that I am true.
And whether I have lost my fight
  Or whether I have won,
I find a faith that I've been right
  As soon as day is done.

The Old-Time Family

It makes me smile to hear 'em tell each other
    nowadays
The burdens they are bearing, with a child or
    two to raise.
Of course the cost of living has gone soaring
    to the sky
And our kids are wearing garments that my par-
    ents couldn't buy.
Now my father wasn't wealthy, but I never
    heard him squeal
Because eight of us were sitting at the table
    every meal.

People fancy they are martyrs if their children
    number three,
And four or five they reckon makes a large-
    sized family.
A dozen hungry youngsters at a table I have
    seen
And their daddy didn't grumble when they
    licked the platter clean.
Oh, I wonder how these mothers and these
    fathers up-to-date
Would like the job of buying little shoes for
    seven or eight.

We were eight around the table in those happy
    days back them,

Eight that cleaned our plates of pot-pie and then
    passed them up again;
Eight that needed shoes and stockings, eight to
    wash and put to bed,
And with mighty little money in the purse, as I
    have said,
But with all the care we brought them, and
    through all the days of stress,
I never heard my father or my mother wish for
    less.

The Job

The job will not make you, my boy;
    The job will not bring you to fame
Or riches or honor or joy
    Or add any weight to your name.
You may fail or succeed where you are,
    May honestly serve or may rob;
        From the start to the end
        Your success will depend
    On just what you make of your job.

Don't look on the job as the thing
    That shall prove what you're able to do;
The job does no more than to bring
    A chance for promotion to you.

Men have shirked in high places and won
  Very justly the jeers of the mob;
    And you'll find it is true
    That it's all up to you
  To say what shall come from the job.

The job is an incident small;
  The thing that's important is man.
The job will not help you at all
  If you won't do the best that you can.
It is you that determines your fate,
  You stand with your hand on the knob
    Of fame's doorway to-day,
    And life asks you to say
  Just what you will make of your job.

Toys

I can pass up the lure of a jewel to wear
  With never the trace of a sigh,
The things on a shelf that I'd like for myself
  I never regret I can't buy.
I can go through the town passing store after
    store
  Showing things it would please me to own,
With never a trace of despair on my face,
  But I can't let a toy shop alone.

I can throttle the love of fine raiment to death
    And I don't know the craving for rum,
But I do know the joy that is born of a toy,
    And the pleasure that comes with a drum.
I can reckon the value of money at times,
    And govern my purse strings with sense,
But I fall for a toy for my girl or my boy
    And never regard the expense.

It's seldom I sigh for unlimited gold
    Or the power of a rich man to buy;
My courage is stout when the doing without
    Is only my duty, but I
Curse the shackles of thrift when I gaze at the
        toys
    That my kiddies are eager to own,
And I'd buy everything that they wish for, by
        Jing!
    If their mother would let me alone.

There isn't much fun spending coin on myself
    For neckties and up-to-date lids,
But there's pleasure tenfold, in the silver and gold
    I part with for things for the kids.
I can go through the town passing store after
        store
    Showing things it would please me to own,
But to thrift I am lost; I won't reckon the cost
    When I'm left in a toy shop alone.

The Mother on the Sidewalk

The mother on the sidewalk as the troops are
    marching by
Is the mother of Old Glory that is waving in
    the sky.
Men have fought to keep it splendid, men have
    died to keep it bright,
But that flag was born of woman and her suf-
    ferings day and night;
'Tis her sacrifice has made it, and once more
    we ought to pray
For the brave and loyal mother of the boy who
    goes away.

There are days of grief before her; there are
    hours that she will weep;
There are nights of anxious waiting when her
    fear will banish sleep;
She has heard her country calling and has risen
    to the test,
And has placed upon the altar of the nation's
    need, her best.
And no man shall ever suffer in the turmoil of
    the fray
The anguish of the mother of the boy who goes
    away.

You may boast men's deeds of glory, you may
    tell their courage great,

But to die is easier service than alone to sit and
    wait,
And I hail the little mother, with the tear-stained
    face and grave,
Who has given the flag a soldier—she's the
    bravest of the brave.
And that banner we are proud of, with its red
    and blue and white,
Is a lasting holy tribute to all mothers' love of
    right.

Memorial Day

The finest tribute we can pay
Unto our hero dead to-day,
Is not a rose wreath, white and red,
In memory of the blood they shed;
It is to stand beside each mound,
Each couch of consecrated ground,
And pledge ourselves as warriors true
Unto the work they died to do.

Into God's valleys where they lie
At rest, beneath the open sky,
Triumphant now o'er every foe,
As living tributes let us go.
No wreath of rose or immortelles
Or spoken word or tolling bells

47

Will do to-day, unless we give
Our pledge that liberty shall live.

Our hearts must be the roses red
We place above our hero dead;
To-day beside their graves we must
Renew allegiance to their trust;
Must bare our heads and humbly say
We hold the Flag as dear as they,
And stand, as once they stood, to die
To keep the Stars and Stripes on high.

The finest tribute we can pay
Unto our hero dead to-day
Is not of speech or roses red,
But living, throbbing hearts instead,
That shall renew the pledge they sealed
With death upon the battlefield:
That freedom's flag shall bear no stain
And free men wear no tyrant's chain.

Memory

I stood and watched him playing,
    A little lad of three,
And back to me came straying
    The years that used to be;

In him the boy was Maying
   Who once belonged to me.

The selfsame brown his eyes were
   As those that once I knew;
As glad and gay his cries were,
   He owned his laughter, too.
His features, form and size were
   My baby's, through and through.

His ears were those I'd sung to;
   His chubby little hands
Were those that I had clung to;
   His hair in golden strands
It seemed my heart was strung to
   By love's unbroken bands.

With him I lived the old days
   That seem so far away;
The beautiful and bold days
   When he was here to play;
The sunny and the gold days
   Of that remembered May.

I know not who he may be
   Nor where his home may be,
But I shall every day be
   In hope again to see
The image of the baby
   Who once belonged to me.

The Stick-Together Families

The stick-together families are happier by far
Than the brothers and the sisters who take separate highways are.
The gladdest people living are the wholesome folks who make
A circle at the fireside that no power but death can break.
And the finest of conventions ever held beneath the sun
Are the little family gatherings when the busy day is done.

There are rich folk, there are poor folk, who imagine they are wise,
And they're very quick to shatter all the little family ties.
Each goes searching after pleasure in his own selected way,
Each with strangers likes to wander, and with strangers likes to play.
But it's bitterness they harvest, and it's empty joy they find,
For the children that are wisest are the stick-together kind.

There are some who seem to fancy that for
    gladness they must roam,
That for smiles that are the brightest they must
    wander far from home.
That the strange friend is the true friend, and
    they travel far astray
And they waste their lives in striving for a joy
    that's far away,
But the gladdest sort of people, when the busy
    day is done,
Are the brothers and the sisters who together
    share their fun.

It's the stick-together family that wins the joys
    of earth,
That hears the sweetest music and that finds the
    finest mirth;
It's the old home roof that shelters all the charm
    that life can give;
There you find the gladdest play-ground, there
    the happiest spot to live.
And, O weary, wandering brother, if content-
    ment you would win,
Come you back unto the fireside and be comrade
    with your kin.

Childless

If certain folks that I know well
Should come to me their woes to tell
I'd read the sorrow in their faces
And I could analyze their cases.
I watch some couples day by day
Go madly on their selfish way
Forever seeking happiness
And always finding something less.
If she whose face is fair to see,
Yet lacks one charm that there should be,
Should open wide her heart to-day
I think I know what she would say.

She'd tell me that his love seems cold
And not the love she knew of old;
That for the home they've built to share
No longer does her husband care;
That he seems happier away
Than by her side, and every day
That passes leaves them more apart;
And then perhaps her tears would start
And in a softened voice she'd add:
"Sometimes I wonder, if we had
A baby now to love, if he
Would find so many faults in me?"

And if he came to tell his woe
Just what he'd say to me, I know:

"There's something dismal in the place
That always stares me in the face.
I love her. She is good and sweet
But still my joy is incomplete.
And then it seems to me that she
Can only see the faults in me.
I wonder sometimes if we had
A little girl or little lad,
If life with all its fret and fuss
Would then seem so monotonous?"

And what I'd say to them I know.
I'd bid them straightway forth to go
And find that child and take him in
And start the joy of life to win.
You foolish, hungry souls, I'd say,
You're living in a selfish way.
A baby's arms stretched out to you
Will give you something real to do.
And though God has not sent one down
To you, within this very town
Somewhere a little baby lies
That would bring gladness to your eyes.

You cannot live this life for gold
Or selfish joys. As you grow old
You'll find that comfort only springs
From living for the living things.
And home must be a barren place
That never knows a baby's face.

Take in a child that needs your care,
Give him your name and let him share
Your happiness and you will own
More joy than you have ever known,
And, what is more, you'll come to feel
That you are doing something real.

The Crucible of Life

Sunshine and shadow, blue sky and gray,
Laughter and tears as we tread on our way;
Hearts that are heavy, then hearts that are light,
Eyes that are misty and eyes that are bright;
Losses and gains in the heat of the strife,
Each in proportion to round out his life.

Into the crucible, stirred by the years,
Go all our hopes and misgivings and fears;
Glad days and sad days, our pleasures and pains,
Worries and comforts, our losses and gains.
Out of the crucible shall there not come
Joy undefiled when we pour off the scum?

Out of the sadness and anguish and woe,
Out of the travail and burdens we know,
Out of the shadow that darkens the way,
Out of the failure that tries us to-day,

Have you a doubt that contentment will come
When you've purified life and discarded the
    scum?

Tinctured with sorrow and flavored with sighs,
Moistened with tears that have flowed from your
    eyes;
Perfumed with sweetness of loves that have died,
Leavened with failures, with grief sanctified,
Sacred and sweet is the joy that must come
From the furnace of life when you've poured off
    the scum.

Unimportant Differences

If he is honest, kindly, true,
    And glad to work from day to day;
If when his bit of toil is through
    With children he will stoop to play;
If he does always what he can
    To serve another's time of need,
Then I shall hail him as a man
    And never ask him what's his creed.

If he respects a woman's name
    And guards her from all thoughtless jeers;
If he is glad to play life's game
    And not risk all to get the cheers;

If he disdains to win by bluff
    And scorns to gain by shady tricks,
I hold that he is good enough
    Regardless of his politics.

If he is glad his much to share
    With them who little here possess,
If he will stand by what is fair
    And not desert to claim success,
If he will leave a smile behind
    As he proceeds from place to place,
He has the proper frame of mind,
    And I won't stop to ask his race.

For when at last life's battle ends
    And all the troops are called on high
We shall discover many friends
    That thoughtlessly we journeyed by.
And we shall learn that God above
    Has judged His creatures by their deeds,
That millions there have won His love
    Who spoke in different tongues and creeds.

The Fishing Outfit

You may talk of stylish raiment,
    You may boast your broadcloth fine,
And the price you gave in payment

May be treble that of mine.
But there's one suit I'd not trade you
    Though it's shabby and it's thin,
For the garb your tailor made you:
        That's the tattered,
        Mud-bespattered
    Suit that I go fishing in.

There's no king in silks and laces
    And with jewels on his breast,
With whom I would alter places.
    There's no man so richly dressed
Or so like a fashion panel
    That, his luxuries to win,
I would swap my shirt of flannel
        And the rusty,
        Frayed and dusty
    Suit that I go fishing in.

'Tis an outfit meant for pleasure;
    It is freedom's raiment, too;
It's a garb that I shall treasure
    Till my time of life is through.
Though perhaps it looks the saddest
    Of all robes for mortal skin,
I am proudest and I'm gladdest
        In that easy,
        Old and greasy
    Suit that I go fishing in.

Grown-Up

Last year he wanted building blocks,
   And picture books and toys,
A saddle horse that gayly rocks,
   And games for little boys.
But now he's big and all that stuff
   His whim no longer suits;
He tells us that he's old enough
   To ask for rubber boots.

Last year whatever Santa brought
   Delighted him to own;
He never gave his wants a thought
   Nor made his wishes known.
But now he says he wants a gun,
   The kind that really shoots,
And I'm confronted with a son
   Demanding rubber boots.

The baby that we used to know
   Has somehow slipped away,
And when or where he chanced to go
   Not one of us can say.
But here's a helter-skelter lad
   That to me nightly scoots
And boldly wishes that he had
   A pair of rubber boots.

I'll bet old Santa Claus will sigh
    When down our flue he comes,
And seeks the babe that used to lie
    And suck his tiny thumbs,
And finds within that little bed
    A grown up boy who hoots
At building blocks, and wants instead
    A pair of rubber boots.

Departed Friends

The dead friends live and always will;
Their presence hovers round us still.
It seems to me they come to share
Each joy or sorrow that we bear.
Among the living I can feel
The sweet departed spirits steal,
And whether it be weal or woe,
I walk with those I used to know.
I can recall them to my side
Whenever I am struggle-tried;
I've but to wish for them, and they
Come trooping gayly down the way,
And I can tell to them my grief
And from their presence find relief.
In sacred memories below
Still live the friends of long ago.

Laughter

Laughter sort o' settles breakfast better than
   digestive pills;
Found it, somehow in my travels, cure for every
   sort of ills;
When the hired help have riled me with their
   slipshod, careless ways,
An' I'm bilin' mad an' cussin' an' my temper's
   all ablaze,
If the calf gets me to laughin' while they're
   teachin' him to feed
Pretty soon I'm feelin' better, 'cause I've found
   the cure I need.

Like to start the day with laughter; when I've had
   a peaceful night,
An' can greet the sun all smilin', that day's goin'
   to be all right.
But there's nothing goes to suit me, when my
   system's full of bile;
Even horses quit their pullin' when the driver
   doesn't smile,
But they'll buckle to the traces when they hear a
   glad giddap,
Just as though they like to labor for a cheerful
   kind o' chap.

Laughter keeps me strong an' healthy. You can
    bet I'm all run down,
Fit for doctor folks an' nurses when I cannot
    shake my frown.
Found in farmin' laughter's useful, good for
    sheep an' cows an' goats;
When I've laughed my way through summer,
    reap the biggest crop of oats.
Laughter's good for any business, leastwise so it
    seems to me—-
Never knew a smilin' feller but was busy as could
    be.

Sometimes sit an' think about it, ponderin' on the
    ways of life,
Wonderin' why mortals gladly face the toil an'
    care an' strife,
Then I come to this conclusion—take it now for
    what it's worth—
It's the joy of laughter keeps us plodding on this
    stretch of earth.
Men the fun o' life are seeking—that's the reason
    for the calf
Spillin' mash upon his keeper—men are hungry
    for a laugh.

The Scoffer

If I had lived in Franklin's time I'm most afraid
    that I,
Beholding him out in the rain, a kite about to fly,
And noticing upon its tail the barn door's rusty
    key,
Would, with the scoffers on the street, have
    chortled in my glee;
And with a sneer upon my lips I would have said
    of Ben,
"His belfry must be full of bats. He's raving,
    boys, again!"

I'm glad I didn't live on earth when Fulton had
    his dream,
And told his neighbors marvelous tales of what
    he'd do with steam,
For I'm not sure I'd not have been a member of
    the throng
That couldn't see how paddle wheels could shove
    a boat along.
At "Fulton's Folly" I'd have sneered, as thou-
    sands did back then,
And called the Clermont's architect the craziest
    of men.

Yet Franklin gave us wonders great and Fulton
    did the same,
And many "boobs" have left behind an everlast-
    ing fame.
And dead are all their scoffers now and all their
    sneers forgot
And scarce a nickel's worth of good was brought
    here by the lot.
I shudder when I stop to think, had I been living
    then,
I might have been a scoffer, too, and jeered at
    Bob and Ben.

I am afraid to-day to sneer at any fellow's dream.
Time was I thought men couldn't fly or sail be-
    neath the stream.
I never call a man a boob who toils throughout
    the night
On visions that I cannot see, because he may be
    right.
I always think of Franklin's trick, which brought
    the jeers of men,
And to myself I say, "Who knows but here's an-
    other Ben?"

The Pathway of the Living

The pathway of the living is our ever-present
care.

Let us do our best to smooth it and to make it
bright and fair;

Let us travel it with kindness, let's be careful as
we tread,

And give unto the living what we'd offer to the
dead.

The pathway of the living we can beautify and
grace;

We can line it deep with roses and make earth a
happier place.

But we've done all mortals can do, when our
prayers are softly said

For the souls of those that travel o'er the pathway of the dead.

The pathway of the living all our strength and
courage needs,

There we ought to sprinkle favors, there we ought
to sow our deeds,

There our smiles should be the brightest, there
our kindest words be said,

For the angels have the keeping of the pathway
of the dead.

Lemon Pie

The world is full of gladness,
   There are joys of many kinds,
There's a cure for every sadness,
   That each troubled mortal finds.
And my little cares grow lighter
   And I cease to fret and sigh,
And my eyes with joy grow brighter
   When she makes a lemon pie.

When the bronze is on the filling
   That's one mass of shining gold,
And its molten joy is spilling
   On the plate, my heart grows bold.
And the kids and I in chorus
   Raise one glad exultant cry
And we cheer the treat before us—
   Which is mother's lemon pie.

Then the little troubles vanish,
   And the sorrows disappear,
Then we find the grit to banish
   All the cares that hovered near,
And we smack our lips in pleasure
   O'er a joy no coin can buy,
And we down the golden treasure
   Which is known as lemon pie.

The Flag on the Farm

We've raised a flagpole on the farm
    And flung Old Glory to the sky,
And it's another touch of charm
    That seems to cheer the passer-by,
But more than that, no matter where
    We're laboring in wood and field,
We turn and see it in the air,
    Our promise of a greater yield.
It whispers to us all day long,
From dawn to dusk: "Be true, be strong;
Who falters now with plow or hoe
Gives comfort to his country's foe."

It seems to me I've never tried
    To do so much about the place,
Nor been so slow to come inside,
    But since I've got the flag to face,
Each night when I come home to rest
    I feel that I must look up there
And say: "Old Flag, I've done my best,
    To-day I've tried to do my share."
And sometimes, just to catch the breeze,
I stop my work, and o'er the trees
Old Glory fairly shouts my way:
"You're shirking far too much to-day!"

The help have caught the spirit, too;
    The hired man takes off his cap

Before the old red, white and blue,
   Then to the horses says: "giddap!"
And starting bravely to the field
   He tells the milkmaid by the door:
"We're going to make these acres yield
   More than they've ever done before."
She smiles to hear his gallant brag,
Then drops a curtsey to the flag.
And in her eyes there seems to shine
A patriotism that is fine.

We've raised a flagpole on the farm
   And flung Old Glory to the sky;
We're far removed from war's alarm,
   But courage here is running high.
We're doing things we never dreamed
   We'd ever find the time to do;
Deeds that impossible once seemed
   Each morning now we hurry through.
The flag now waves above our toil
And sheds its glory on the soil,
And boy and man looks up to it
As if to say: "I'll do my bit!"

Heroes

There are different kinds of heroes, there are
  some you hear about.
They get their pictures printed, and their names
  the newsboys shout;
There are heroes known to glory that were not
  afraid to die
In the service of their country and to keep the
  flag on high;
There are brave men in the trenches, there are
  brave men on the sea,
But the silent, quiet heroes also prove their
  bravery.

I am thinking of a hero that was never known
  to fame,
Just a manly little fellow with a very common
  name;
He was freckle-faced and ruddy, but his head
  was nobly shaped,
And he one day took the whipping that his comrades all escaped.
And he never made a murmur, never whimpered
  in reply;
He would rather take the censure than to stand
  and tell a lie.

And I'm thinking of another that had courage
    that was fine,
And I've often wished in moments that such
    strength of will were mine.
He stood against his comrades, and he left them
    then and there
When they wanted him to join them in a deed
    that wasn't fair.
He stood alone, undaunted, with his little head
    erect;
He would rather take the jeering than to lose
    his self-respect.

And I know a lot of others that have grown
    to manhood now,
Who have yet to wear the laurel that adorns the
    victor's brow.
They have plodded on in honor through the dusty,
    dreary ways,
They have hungered for life's comforts and the
    joys of easy days,
But they've chosen to be toilers, and in this their
    splendor's told:
They would rather never have it than to do some
    things for gold.

The Mother's Question

When I was a boy, and it chanced to rain,
  Mother would always watch for me;
She used to stand by the window pane,
  Worried and troubled as she could be.
And this was the question I used to hear,
The very minute that I drew near;
The words she used, I can't forget:
"Tell me, my boy, if your feet are wet."

Worried about me was mother dear,
  As healthy a lad as ever strolled
Over a turnpike, far or near,
  'Fraid to death that I'd take a cold.
Always stood by the window pane,
Watching for me in the pouring rain;
And her words in my ears are ringing yet:
"Tell me, my boy, if your feet are wet."

Stockings warmed by the kitchen fire,
  And slippers ready for me to wear;
Seemed that mother would never tire,
  Giving her boy the best of care,
Thinking of him the long day through,
In the worried way that all mothers do;
Whenever it rained she'd start to fret,
Always fearing my feet were wet.

And now, whenever it rains, I see
  A vision of mother in days of yore,
Still waiting there to welcome me,
  As she used to do by the open door.
And always I think as I enter there
Of a mother's love and a mother's care;
Her words in my ears are ringing yet:
"Tell me, my boy, if your feet are wet."

The Blue Flannel Shirt

I am eager once more to feel easy,
  I'm weary of thinking of dress;
I'm heartily sick of stiff collars,
  And trousers the tailor must press.
I'm eagerly waiting the glad days—
When fashion will cease to assert
What I must put on every morning —
The days of the blue flannel shirt.

I want to get out in the country
  And rest by the side of the lake;
To go a few days without shaving,
  And give grim old custom the shake.
A week's growth of whiskers, I'm thinking,
At present my chin wouldn't hurt;

And I'm yearning to don those old trousers
And loaf in that blue flannel shirt.

You can brag all you like of your fashions,
The style of your cutaway coat;
You can boast of your tailor-made raiment,
And the collar that strangles your throat;
But give me the old pair of trousers
That seem to improve with the dirt,
And let me get back to the comfort
That's born of a blue flannel shirt.

Grandpa

My grandpa is the finest man
Excep' my pa. My grandpa can
Make kites an' carts an' lots of things
You pull along the ground with strings,
And he knows all the names of birds,
And how they call 'thout using words,
And where they live and what they eat,
And how they build their nests so neat.
He's lots of fun! Sometimes all day
He comes to visit me and play.
You see he's getting old, and so
To work he doesn't have to go,
And when it isn't raining, he
Drops in to have some fun with me.

He takes my hand and we go out
And everything we talk about.
He tells me how God makes the trees,
And why it hurts to pick up bees.
Sometimes he stops and shows to me
The place where fairies used to be;
And then he tells me stories, too,
And I am sorry when he's through.
When I am asking him for more
He says: "Why there's a candy store!
Let's us go there and see if they
Have got the kind we like to-day."
Then when we get back home my ma
Says: "You are spoiling Buddy, Pa."

My grandpa is my mother's pa,
I guess that's what all grandpas are.
And sometimes ma, all smiles, will say:
"You didn't always act that way.
When I was little, then you said
That children should be sent to bed
And not allowed to rule the place
And lead old folks a merry chase."
And grandpa laughs and says: "That's true,
That's what I used to say to you.
It is a father's place to show
The young the way that they should go,
But grandpas have a different task,
Which is to get them all they ask."

73

When I get big and old and gray
I'm going to spend my time in play;
I'm going to be a grandpa, too,
And do as all the grandpas do.
I'll buy my daughter's children things
Like horns and drums and tops with strings,
And tell them all about the trees
And frogs and fish and birds and bees
And fairies in the shady glen
And tales of giants, too, and when
They beg of me for just one more,
I'll take them to the candy store;
I'll buy them everything they see
The way my grandpa does for me

Pa Did It

The train of cars that Santa brought is out of
      kilter now;
While pa was showing how they went he broke
      the spring somehow.
They used to run around a track—at least they
      did when he
Would let me take them in my hands an' wind 'em
      with a key.

I could 'a' had some fun with 'em, if only they
would go,
But, gee! I never had a chance, for pa enjoyed
'em so.

The automobile that I got that ran around the
floor
Was lots of fun when it was new, but it won't
go no more.
Pa wound it up for Uncle Jim to show him how
it went,
And when those two got through with it the
runnin' gear was bent,
An' now it doesn't go at all.   I mustn't grumble
though,
'Cause while it was in shape to run my pa enjoyed
it so.

I've got my blocks as good as new, my mitts are
perfect yet;
Although the snow is on the ground I haven't got
'em wet.
I've taken care of everything that Santa brought
to me,
Except the toys that run about when wound up
with a key.
But next year you can bet I won't make any such
mistake;
I'm going to ask for toys an' things that my pa
cannot break.

The Real Successes

You think that the failures are many,
  You think the successes are few,
But you judge by the rule of the penny,
  And not by the good that men do.
You judge men by standards of treasure
  That merely obtain upon earth,
When the brother you're snubbing may measure
  Full-length to God's standard of worth.

The failures are not in the ditches,
  The failures are not in the ranks,
They have missed the acquirement of riches,
  Their fortunes are not in the banks.
Their virtues are never paraded,
  Their worth is not always in view,
But they're fighting their battles unaided,
  And fighting them honestly, too.

There are failures to-day in high places
  The failures aren't all in the low;
There are rich men with scorn in their faces
  Whose homes are but castles of woe.
The homes that are happy are many,
  And numberless fathers are true;
And this is the standard, if any,
  By which we must judge what men do.

Wherever loved ones are awaiting
   The toiler to kiss and caress,
Though in Bradstreet's he hasn't a rating,
   He still is a splendid success.
If the dear ones who gather about him
   And know what he's striving to do
Have never a reason to doubt him,
   Is he less successful than you?

You think that the failures are many,
   You judge by men's profits in gold;
You judge by the rule of the penny—
   In this true success isn't told.
This falsely man's story is telling,
   For wealth often brings on distress,
But wherever love brightens a dwelling,
   There lives, rich or poor, a success.

The Sorry Hostess

She said she was sorry the weather was bad
The night that she asked us to dine;
And she really appeared inexpressibly sad
Because she had hoped 'twould be fine.
She was sorry to hear that my wife had a cold,
And she almost shed tears over that,
And how sorry she was, she most feelingly told,
That the steam wasn't on in the flat.

She was sorry she hadn't asked others to come,
She might just as well have had eight;
She said she was downcast and terribly glum
Because her dear husband was late.
She apologized then for the home she was in,
For the state of the rugs and the chairs,
For the children who made such a horrible din,
And then for the squeak in the stairs.

When the dinner began she apologized twice
For the olives, because they were small;
She was certain the celery, too, wasn't nice,
And the soup didn't suit her at all.
She was sorry she couldn't get whitefish instead
Of the trout that the fishmonger sent,
But she hoped that we'd manage somehow to be
         fed,
Though her dinner was not what she meant.

She spoke her regrets for the salad, and then
Explained she was really much hurt,
And begged both our pardons again and again
For serving a skimpy dessert.
She was sorry for this and sorry for that,
Though there really was nothing to blame.
But I thought to myself as I put on my hat,
Perhaps she is sorry we came.

Yesterday

I've trod the links with many a man,
　　And played him club for club;
'Tis scarce a year since I began
　　And I am still a dub.
But this I've noticed as we strayed
　　Along the bunkered way,
No one with me has ever played
　　As he did yesterday.

It makes no difference what the drive,
　　Together as we walk,
Till we up to the ball arrive,
　　I get the same old talk:
"To-day there's something wrong with me.
　　Just what I cannot say.

Would you believe I got a three
  For this hole—yesterday?"

I see them top and slice a shot,
  And fail to follow through,
And with their brassies plough the lot,
  The very way I do.
To six and seven their figures run,
  And then they sadly say:
"I neither dubbed nor foozled one
  When I played—yesterday."

I have no yesterdays to count,
  No good work to recall;
Each morning sees hope proudly mount,
  Each evening sees it fall.
And in the locker room at night,
  When men discuss their play,
I hear them and I wish I might
  Have seen them—yesterday.

Oh, dear old yesterday! What store
  Of joys for men you hold!
I'm sure there is no day that's more
  Remembered or extolled.
I'm off my task myself a bit,
  My mind has run astray;
I think, perhaps, I should have writ
  These verses—yesterday.

The Beauty Places

Here she walked and romped about,
    And here beneath this apple tree
Where all the grass is trampled out
    The swing she loved so used to be.
This path is but a path to you,
Because my child you never knew.

'Twas here she used to stoop to smell
    The first bright daffodil of spring;
'Twas here she often tripped and fell
    And here she heard the robins sing.
You'd call this but a common place,
But you have never seen her face.

And it was here we used to meet.
    How beautiful a spot is this,
To which she gayly raced to greet
    Her daddy with his evening kiss!
You see here nothing grand or fine,
But, Oh, what memories are mine!

The people pass from day to day
    And never turn their heads to see
The many charms along the way
    That mean so very much to me.
For all things here are speaking of
The babe that once was mine to love

The Little Old Man

The little old man with the curve in his back
And the eyes that are dim and the skin that is
    slack,
So slack that it wrinkles and rolls on his cheeks,
With a thin little voice that goes "crack!" when
    he speaks,
Never goes to the store but that right at his feet
Are all of the youngsters who live on the street.

And the little old man in the suit that was black,
And once might have perfectly fitted his back,
Has a boy's chubby fist in his own wrinkled hand,
And together they trudge off to Light-Hearted
    Land;
Some splendid excursions he gives every day
To the boys and the girls in his funny old way.

The little old man is as queer as can be;
He'd spend all his time with a child on his knee;
And the stories he tells I could never repeat,
But they're always of good boys and little girls
    sweet;
And the children come home at the end of the day
To tell what the little old man had to say.

Once the little old man didn't trudge to the store,
And the tap of his cane wasn't heard any more;
The children looked eagerly for him each day

And wondered why he didn't come out to play
Till some of them saw Doctor Brown ring his bell,
And they wept when they heard that he might
    not get well.

But after awhile he got out with his cane,
And called all the children around him again;
And I think as I see him go trudging along
In the center, once more, of his light-hearted
    throng,
That earth has no glory that's greater than this:
The little old man whom the children would miss.

The Little Velvet Suit

Last night I got to thinkin' of the pleasant long
    ago,
When I still had on knee breeches, an' I wore a
    flowing bow,
An' my Sunday suit was velvet. Ma an' Pa
    thought it was fine,
But I know I didn't like it—either velvet or
    design;
It was far too girlish for me, for I wanted some-
    thing rough
Like what other boys were wearing, but Ma
    wouldn't buy such stuff.

Ma answered all my protests in her sweet an'
    kindly way;
She said it didn't matter what I wore to run an'
    play,
But on Sundays when all people went to church
    an' wore their best,
Her boy must look as stylish an' as well kept as
    the rest.
So she dressed me up in velvet, an' she tied the
    flowing bow,
An' she straightened out my stockings, so that
    not a crease would show.

An' then I chuckled softly to myself while dream-
    ing there
An' I saw her standing o'er me combing out my
    tangled hair.
I could feel again the tugging, an' I heard the
    yell I gave
When she struck a snarl, an' softly I could hear
    her say: "Be brave.
'Twill be over in a minute, and a little man like
    you
Shouldn't whimper at a little bit of pain the way
    you do."

Oh, I wouldn't mind the tugging at my scalp lock,
    and I know
That I'd gladly wear to please her that old flow-
    ing girlish bow;

And I think I'd even try to don once more that
    velvet suit,
And blush the same old blushes, as the women
    called me cute,
Could the dear old mother only take me by the
    hand again,
And be as proud of me right now as she was
    always then.

The First Steps

Last night I held my arms to you
And you held yours to mine
And started out to march to me
As any soldier fine.
You lifted up your little feet
And laughingly advanced;
And I stood there and gazed upon
Your first wee steps, entranced.

You gooed and gurgled as you came
Without a sign of fear;
As though you knew, your journey o'er,
I'd greet you with a cheer.
And, what is more, you seemed to know,
Although you are so small,
That I was there, with eager arms,
To save you from a fall.

Three tiny steps you took, and then,
Disaster and dismay!
Your over-confidence had led
Your little feet astray.
You did not see what we could see
Nor fear what us alarms;
You stumbled, but ere you could fall
I caught you in my arms.

You little tyke, in days to come
You'll bravely walk alone,
And you may have to wander paths
Where dangers lurk unknown.
And, Oh, I pray that then, as now,
When accidents befall
You'll still remember that I'm near
To save you from a fall.

Signs

It's "be a good boy, Willie,"
    And it's "run away and play,
For Santa Slaus is coming
    With his reindeer and his sleigh."
It's "mind what mother tells you,"
    And it's "put away your toys,
For Santa Claus is coming
    To the good girls and the boys."

Ho, Santa Claus is coming, there is Christmas in
the air,
And little girls and little boys are good now
everywhere.

World-wide the little fellows
Now are sweetly saying "please,"
And "thank you," and "excuse me,"
And those little pleasantries
That good children are supposed to
When there's company to hear;
And it's just as plain as can be
That the Christmas time is near.
Ho, it's just as plain as can be that old Santa's
on his way,
For there are no little children that are really bad
to-day.

And when evening shadows lengthen,
Every little curly head
Now is ready, aye, and willing
To be tucked away in bed;
Not one begs to stay up longer,
Not one even sheds a tear;
Ho, the goodness of the children
Is a sign that Santa's near.
It's wonderful, the goodness of the little tots
to-day,
When they know that good old Santa has begun
to pack his sleigh.

The Family's Homely Man

There never was a family without its homely
    man,
With legs a little longer than the ordinary plan,
An' a shock of hair that brush an' comb can't ever
    straighten out,
An' hands that somehow never seem to know
    what they're about;
The one with freckled features and a nose that
    looks as though
It was fashioned by the youngsters from a chunk
    of mother's dough.
You know the man I'm thinking of, the homely
    one an' plain,
That fairly oozes kindness like a rosebush drip-
    ping rain.
His face is never much to see, but back of it there
    lies
A heap of love and tenderness and judgment,
    sound and wise.

And so I sing the homely man that's sittin' in his
    chair,
And pray that every family will always have him
    there.
For looks don't count for much on earth; it's
    hearts that wear the gold;
An' only that is ugly which is selfish, cruel, cold.

The family needs him, Oh, so much; more, maybe, than they know;
Folks seldom guess a man's real worth until he has to go,
But they will miss a heap of love an' tenderness the day
God beckons to their homely man, an' he must go away.

He's found in every family, it doesn't matter where
They live or be they rich or poor, the homely man is there.
You'll find him sitting quiet-like and sort of drawn apart,
As though he felt he shouldn't be where folks are fine an' smart.
He likes to hide himself away, a watcher of the fun,
An' seldom takes a leading part when any game's begun.
But when there's any task to do, like need for extra chairs,
I've noticed it's the homely man that always climbs the stairs.

And always it's the homely man that happens in to mend
The little toys the youngsters break, for he's the children's friend.

And he's the one that sits all night to watch beside
    the dead,
And sends the worn-out sorrowers and broken
    hearts to bed.
The family wouldn't be complete without him
    night or day,
To smooth the little troubles out and drive the
    cares away.

When Mother Cooked with Wood

I do not quarrel with the gas,
    Our modern range is fine,
The ancient stove was doomed to pass
    From Time's grim firing line,
Yet now and then there comes to me
    The thought of dinners good
And pies and cake that used to be
    When mother cooked with wood.

The axe has vanished from the yard,
    The chopping block is gone,
There is no pile of cordwood hard
    For boys to work upon;
There is no box that must be filled
    Each morning to the hood;
Time in its ruthlessness has willed
    The passing of the wood.

And yet those days were fragrant days
　And spicy days and rare;
The kitchen knew a cheerful blaze
　And friendliness was there.
And every appetite was keen
　For breakfasts that were good
When I had scarcely turned thirteen
　And mother cooked with wood.

I used to dread my daily chore,
　I used to think it tough
When mother at the kitchen door
　Said I'd not chopped enough.
And on her baking days, I know,
　I shirked whene'er I could
In that now happy long ago
　When mother cooked with wood.

I never thought I'd wish to see
　That pile of wood again;
Back then it only seemed to me
　A source of care and pain.
But now I'd gladly give my all
　To stand where once I stood,
If those rare days I could recall
　When mother cooked with wood.

Midnight in the Pantry

You can boast your round of pleasures, praise
the sound of popping corks,
Where the orchestra is playing to the rattle of
the forks;
And your after-opera dinner you may think
superbly fine,
But that can't compare, I'm certain, to the joy
that's always mine
When I reach my little dwelling—source of all
sincere delight—
And I prowl around the pantry in the waning
hours of night.

When my business, or my pleasure, has detained
me until late,
And it's midnight, say, or after, when I reach my
own estate,
Though I'm weary with my toiling I don't hustle
up to bed,
For the inner man is hungry and he's anxious to
be fed;
Then I feel a thrill of glory from my head down
to my feet
As I prowl around the pantry after something
good to eat.

Oft I hear a call above me: "Goodness gracious,
come to bed!"
And I know that I've disturbed her by my over-
eager tread,
But I've found a glass of jelly and some bread
and butter, too,
And a bit of cold fried chicken and I answer:
"When I'm through!"
Oh, there's no cafe that better serves my precious
appetite
Than the pantry in our kitchen when I get home
late at night.

You may boast your shining silver, and the linen
and the flowers,
And the music and the laughter and the lights
that hang in showers;
You may have your cafe table with its brilliant
array,
But it doesn't charm yours truly when I'm on my
homeward way;
For a greater joy awaits me, as I hunger for a
bite—
Just the joy of pantry-prowling in the middle of
the night.

The World Is Against Me

"The world is against me," he said with a sigh
"Somebody stops every scheme that I try..
The world has me down and it's keeping me there;
I don't get a chance. Oh, the world is unfair!
When a fellow is poor then he can't get a show;
The world is determined to keep him down low."

"What of Abe Lincoln?" I asked. "Would you
    say
That he was much richer than you are to-day?
He hadn't your chance of making his mark,
And his outlook was often exceedingly dark;
Yet he clung to his purpose with courage most
    grim
And he got to the top. Was the world against
    him?"

"What of Ben Franklin? I've oft heard it said
That many a time he went hungry to bed.
He started with nothing but courage to climb,
But patiently struggled and waited his time.
He dangled awhile from real poverty's limb,
Yet he got to the top. Was the world against him?

"I could name you a dozen, yes, hundreds, I guess,
Of poor boys who've patiently climbed to success;
All boys who were down and who struggled alone,

Who'd have thought themselves rich if your for-
    tune they'd known;
Yet they rose in the world you're so quick to
    condemn,
And I'm asking you now, was the world against
    them?"

Bribed

I know that what I did was wrong;
    I should have sent you far away.
You tempted me, and I'm not strong;
    I tried but couldn't answer nay.
I should have packed you off to bed;
    Instead I let you stay awhile,
And mother scolded when I said
    That you had bribed me with your smile.

And yesterday I gave to you
    Another piece of chocolate cake,
Some red-ripe watermelon, too,
    And that gave you the stomach ache.
And that was after I'd been told
    You'd had enough, you saucy miss;
You tempted me, you five-year-old,
    And bribed me with a hug and kiss.

And mother said I mustn't get
   You roller skates, yet here they are;
I haven't dared to tell her yet;
   Some time, she says, I'll go too far.
I gave my word I wouldn't buy
   These things, for accidents she fears;
Now I must tell, when questioned why,
   Just how you bribed me with your tears.

I've tried so hard to do the right,
   Yet I have broken every vow.
I let you do, most every night,
   The things your mother won't allow.
I know that I am doing wrong,
   Yet all my sense of honor flies,
The moment that you come along
   And bribe me with those wondrous eyes.

The Home Builders

The world is filled with bustle and with selfishness
   and greed,
It is filled with restless people that are dreaming
   of a deed.
You can read it in their faces; they are dreaming
   of the day
When they'll come to fame and fortune and put
   all their cares away.

And I think as I behold them, though it's far
    indeed they roam,
They will never find contentment save they seek
    for it at home.

I watch them as they hurry through the surging
    lines of men,
Spurred to speed by grim ambition, and I know
    they're dreaming then.
They are weary, sick and footsore, but their go-
    seems far away,
And it's little they've accomplished at the ending
    of the day.
It is rest they're vainly seeking, love and laugh-
    ter in the gloam,
But they'll never come to claim it, save they claim
    it here at home.

For the peace that is the sweetest isn't born of
    minted gold,
And the joy that lasts the longest and still lingers
    when we're old
Is no dim and distant pleasure—it is not to-mor-
    row's prize,
It is not the end of toiling, or the rainbow of our
    sighs.
It is every day within us—all the rest is hippo-
    drome—
And the soul that is the gladdest is the soul that
    builds a home.

They are fools who build for glory! They are
    fools who pin their hopes
On the come and go of battles or some vessel's
    slender ropes.
They shall sicken and shall wither and shall never
    peace attain
Who believe that real contentment only men vic- ·
    torious gain.
For the only happy toilers under earth's majestic
    dome
Are the ones who find their glories in the little
    spot called home.

My Books and I

My books and I are good old pals:
    My laughing books are gay,
Just suited for my merry moods
    When I am wont to play.
Bill Nye comes down to joke with me
    And, Oh, the joy he spreads.
Just like two fools we sit and laugh
    And shake our merry heads.

When I am in a thoughtful mood,
    With Stevenson I sit,
Who seems to know I've had enough
    Of Bill Nye and his wit.

And so, more thoughtful than I am,
　　He talks of lofty things,
And thus an evening hour we spend
　　Sedate and grave as kings.

And should my soul be torn with grief
　　Upon my shelf I find
A little volume, torn and thumbled,
　　For comfort just designed.
I take my little Bible down
　　And read its pages o'er,
And when I part from it I find
　　I'm stronger than before.

Success

I hold no dream of fortune vast,
　　Nor seek undying fame.
I do not ask when life is past
　　That many know my name.

I may not own the skill to rise
　　To glory's topmost height,
Nor win a place among the wise,
　　But I can keep the right.

And I can live my life on earth
　　Contented to the end,
If but a few shall know my worth
　　And proudly call me friend.

Questions

Would you sell your boy for a stack of gold?
Would you miss that hand that is yours to hold?
Would you take a fortune and never see
The man, in a few brief years, he'll be?
Suppose that his body were racked with pain,
How much would you pay for his health again?

Is there money enough in the world to-day
To buy your boy?   Could a monarch pay
You silver and gold in so large a sum
That you'd have him blinded or stricken dumb?
How much would you take, if you had the choice,
Never to hear, in this world, his voice?

How much would you take in exchange for all
The joy that is wrapped in that youngster small?
Are there diamonds enough in the mines of earth
To equal your dreams of that youngster's worth?
Would you give up the hours that he's on your
        knee
The richest man in the world to be?

You may prate of gold, but your fortune lies,
And you know it well, in your boy's bright eyes.
And there's nothing that money can buy or do
That means so much as that boy to you.
Well, which does the most of your time employ,
The chase for gold—or that splendid boy?

Sausage

You may brag about your breakfast foods you
    eat at break of day,
Your crisp, delightful shavings and your stack of
    last year's hay,
Your toasted flakes of rye and corn that fairly
    swim in cream,
Or rave about a sawdust mash, an epicurean
    dream.
But none of these appeals to me, though all of
    them I've tried—
The breakfast that I liked the best was sausage
    mother fried.

Old country sausage was its name; the kind, of
    course, you know,
The little links that seemed to be almost as white
    as snow,
But turned unto a ruddy brown, while sizzling in
    the pan;
Oh, they were made both to appease and charm
    the inner man.
All these new-fangled dishes make me blush and
    turn aside,
When I think about the sausage that for break-
    fast mother fried.

When they roused me from my slumbers and I
    left to do the chores,

It wasn't long before I breathed a fragrance out
of doors
That seemed to grip my spirit, and to thrill my
body through,
For the spice of hunger tingled, and 'twas then I
plainly knew
That the gnawing at my stomach would be quickly
satisfied
By a plate of country sausage that my dear old
mother fried.

There upon the kitchen table, with its cloth of
turkey red,
Was a platter heaped with sausage and a plate of
home-made bread,
And a cup of coffee waiting—not a puny demi-
tasse
That can scarcely hold a mouthful, but a cup of
greater class;
And I fell to eating largely, for I could not be
denied—
Oh, I'm sure a king would relish the sausage
mother fried.

Times have changed and so have breakfasts; now
each morning when I see
A dish of shredded something or of flakes passed
up to me,
All my thoughts go back to boyhood, to the days
of long ago,

When the morning meal meant something more
    than vain and idle show.
And I hunger, Oh, I hunger, in a way I cannot
    hide,
For a plate of steaming sausage like the kind my
    mother fried.

Friends

Ain't it fine when things are going
    Topsy-turvy and askew
To discover someone showing
    Good old-fashioned faith in you?

Ain't it good when life seems dreary
    And your hopes about to end,
Just to feel the handclasp cheery
    Of a fine old loyal friend?

Gosh! one fellow to another
    Means a lot from day to day,
Seems we're living for each other
    In a friendly sort of way.

When a smile or cheerful greetin'
    Means so much to fellows sore,
Seems we ought to keep repeatin'
    Smiles an' praises more an' more.

A Boost for Modern Methods

In some respects the old days were perhaps ahead
    of these,
Before we got to wanting wealth and costly
    luxuries;
Perhaps the world was happier then, I'm not the
    one to say,
But when it's zero weather I am glad I live to-day.

Old-fashioned winters I recall—the winters of
    my youth—
I have no great desire for them to-day, I say in
    truth;
The frost upon the window panes was beautiful
    to see,
But the chill upon that bedroom floor was not a
    joy to me.

I do not now recall that it was fun in those days
    when
I woke to learn the water pipes were frozen tight
    "again."
To win once more the old-time joys, I don't
    believe I'd care
To have to sleep, for comfort's sake, dressed in
    my underwear.

Old-fashioned winters had their charms, a fact I
  can't deny,
But after all I'm really glad that they have wandered by;
We used to tumble out of bed, like firemen, I
  declare,
And grab our clothes and hike down stairs and
  finish dressing there.

Yes, brag about those days of old, boast of them
  as you will,
I sing the modern methods that have robbed them
  of their chill;
I sing the cheery steam pipe and the upstairs
  snug and warm
And a spine that's free from shivers as I robe
  my manly form.

The Man to Be

Some day the world will need a man of courage
in a time of doubt,
And somewhere, as a little boy, that future hero
plays about.
Within some humble home, no doubt, that instru-
ment of greater things
Now climbs upon his father's knee or to his
mother's garments clings.
And when shall come that call for him to render
service that is fine,
He that shall do God's mission here may be your
little boy or mine.

Long years of preparation mark the pathway for
the splendid souls,
And generations live and die and seem no nearer
to their goals,
And yet the purpose of it all, the fleeting pleasure
and the woe,
The laughter and the grief of life that all who
come to earth must know
May be to pave the way for one—one man to
serve the Will Divine
And it is possible that he may be your little boy
or mine.

Some day the world will need a man! I stand
beside his cot at night
And wonder if I'm teaching him, as best I can,
to know the right.
I am the father of a boy—his life is mine to
make or mar—
And he no better can become than what my daily
teachings are;
There will be need for someone great—I dare
not falter from the line—
The man that is to serve the world may be that
little boy of mine.

Perhaps your boy and mine may not ascend the
lofty heights of fame;
The orders for their births are hid. We know
not why to earth they came.
Yet in some little bed to-night the great man of
to-morrow sleeps
And only He who sent him here, the secret of his
purpose keeps.
As fathers then our care is this—to keep in mind
the Great Design.
The man the world shall need some day may be
your little boy or mine.

The Summer Children

I like 'em in the winter when their cheeks are
 slightly pale,
I like 'em in the spring time when the March
 winds blow a gale;
But when summer suns have tanned 'em and
 they're racing to and fro,
I somehow think the children make the finest
 sort of show.

When they're brown as little berries and they're
 bare of foot and head,
And they're on the go each minute where the
 velvet lawns are spread,
Then their health is at its finest and they never
 stop to rest,
Oh, it's then I think the children look and are
 their very best.

We've got to know the winter and we've got to
 know the spring,
But for children, could I do it, unto summer I
 would cling;
For I'm happiest when I see 'em, as a wild and
 merry band
Of healthy, lusty youngsters that the summer
 sun has tanned.

October

Days are gettin' shorter an' the air a keener snap;
Apples now are droppin' into Mother Nature's
    lap;
The mist at dusk is risin' over valley, marsh an'
    fen
An' it's just as plain as sunshine, winter's comin
    on again.

The turkeys now are struttin' round the old farm-
    house once more;
They are done with all their nestin', and their
    hatchin' days are o'er;
Now the farmer's cuttin' fodder for the silo
    towerin' high
An' he's frettin' an' complainin' 'cause the corn's
    a bit too dry.

But the air is mighty peaceful an' the scene is
    good to see,
An' there's somethin' in October that stirs deep
    inside o' me;
An' I just can't help believin' in a God above us
    when
Everything is ripe for harvest an' the frost is
    back again.

On Quitting

How much grit do you think you've got?
Can you quit a thing that you like a lot?
You may talk of pluck; it's an easy word,
And where'er you go it is often heard;
But can you tell to a jot or guess
Just how much courage you now possess?

You may stand to trouble and keep your grin,
But have you tackled self-discipline?
Have you ever issued commands to you
To quit the things that you like to do,
And then, when tempted and sorely swayed,
Those rigid orders have you obeyed?

Don't boast of your grit till you've tried it out,
Nor prate to men of your courage stout,
For it's easy enough to retain a grin
In the face of a fight there's a chance to win,
But the sort of grit that is good to own
Is the stuff you need when you're all alone.

How much grit do you think you've got?
Can you turn from joys that you like a lot?
Have you ever tested yourself to know
How far with yourself your will can go?
If you want to know if you have grit,
Just pick out a joy that you like, and quit.

It's bully sport and it's open fight;
It will keep you busy both day and night;
For the toughest kind of a game you'll find
Is to make your body obey your mind.
And you never will know what is meant by grit
Unless there's something you've tried to quit.

The Price of Riches

Nobody stops at the rich man's door to pass the
time of day.
Nobody shouts a "hello!" to him in the good old-
fashioned way.
Nobody comes to his porch at night and sits in
that extra chair
And talks till it's time to go to bed. He's all by
himself up there.

Nobody just happens in to call on the long, cold
winter nights.
Nobody feels that he's welcome now, though the
house is ablaze with lights.
And never an unexpected guest will tap at his
massive door
And stay to tea as he used to do, for his neigh-
borly days are o'er.

It's a distant life that the rich man leads and many
an hour is glum,
For never the neighbors call on him save when
they are asked to come.
At heart he is just as he used to be and he longs
for his friends of old,
But they never will venture unbidden there.
They're afraid of his wall of gold.

For silver and gold in a large amount there's a
price that all men must pay,
And who will dwell in a rich man's house must
live in a lonely way.
For once you have builded a fortune vast you
will sigh for the friends you knew
But never they'll tap at your door again in the
way that they used to do.

The Other Fellow

Whose luck is better far than ours?
The other fellow's.
Whose road seems always lined with flowers?
The other fellow's.
Who is the man who seems to get
Most joy in life, with least regret,
Who always seems to win his bet?
The other fellow.

Who fills the place we think we'd like?
The other fellow.
Whom does good fortune always strike?
The other fellow.
Whom do we envy, day by day?
Who has more time than we to play?
Who is it, when we mourn, seems gay?
The other fellow.

Who seems to miss the thorns we find?
The other fellow.
Who seems to leave us all behind?
The other fellow.
Who never seems to feel the woe,
The anguish and the pain we know?
Who gets the best seats at the show?
The other fellow.

And yet, my friend, who envies you?
The other fellow.
Who thinks he gathers only rue?
The other fellow.
Who sighs because he thinks that he
Would infinitely happier be,
If he could be like you or me?
The other fellow.

The Open Fire

There in the flame of the open grate,
  All that is good in the past I see:
Red-lipped youth on the swinging gate,
  Bright-eyed youth with its minstrelsy;
    Girls and boys that I used to know,
    Back in the days of Long Ago,
Troop before in the smoke and flame,
  Chatter and sing, as the wild birds do.
Everyone I can call by name,
  For the fire builds all of my youth anew.

Outside, people go stamping by,
  Squeak of wheel on the evening air,
Stars and planets race through the sky,
  Here are darkness and silence rare;
    Only the flames in the open grate
    Crackle and flare as they burn up hate,
Malice and envy and greed for gold,
  Dancing, laughing my cares away;
I've forgotten that I am old,
  Once again I'm a boy at play.

There in the flame of the open grate
  Bright the pictures come and go;
Lovers swing on the garden gate,
  Lovers kiss 'neath the mistletoe.
    I've forgotten that I am old,
    I've forgotten my story's told;

Whistling boy down the lane I stroll,
All untouched by the blows of fate,
Time turns back and I'm young of soul,
Dreaming there by the open grate.

Improvement

The joy of life is living it, or so it seems to me;
In finding shackles on your wrists, then struggling
　　till you're free;
In seeing wrongs and righting them, in dreaming
　　splendid dreams,
Then toiling till the vision is as real as moving
　　streams.
The happiest mortal on the earth is he who ends
　　his day
By leaving better than he found to bloom along
　　the way.

Were all things perfect here there would be
　　naught for man to do;
If what is old were good enough we'd never need
　　the new.
The only happy time of rest is that which follows
　　strife
And sees some contribution made unto the joy of
　　life.

And he who has oppression felt and conquered it
    is he
Who really knows the happiness and peace of
    being free.

The miseries of earth are here and with them all
    must cope.
Who seeks for joy, through hedges thick of care
    and pain must grope.
Through disappointment man must go to value
    pleasure's thrill;
To really know the joy of health a man must first
    be ill.
The wrongs are here for man to right, and happi-
    ness is had
By striving to supplant with good the evil and the
    bad.

The joy of life is living it and doing things of
    worth,
In making bright and fruitful all the barren spots
    of earth.
In facing odds and mastering them and rising
    from defeat,
And making true what once was false, and what
    was bitter, sweet.
For only he knows perfect joy whose little bit of
    soil
Is richer ground than what it was when he began
    to toil.

Send Her a Valentine

Send her a valentine to say
You love her in the same old way.
Just drop the long familiar ways
And live again the old-time days
When love was new and youth was bright
And all was laughter and delight,
And treat her as you would if she
Were still the girl that used to be.

Pretend that all the years have passed
Without one cold and wintry blast;
That you are coming still to woo
Your sweetheart as you used to do;
Forget that you have walked along
The paths of life where right and wrong
And joy and grief in battle are,
And play the heart without a scar.

Be what you were when youth was fine
And send to her a valentine;
Forget the burdens and the woe
That have been given you to know
And to the wife, so fond and true,
The pledges of the past renew.
'Twill cure her life of every ill
To find that you're her sweetheart still.

Bud

Who is it lives to the full every minute,
Gets all the joy and the fun that is in it?
Tough as they make 'em, and ready to race,
Fit for a battle and fit for a chase,
Heedless of buttons on blouses and pants,
Laughing at danger and taking a chance,
Gladdest, it seems, when he wallows in mud,
Who is the rascal? I'll tell you, it's Bud!

Who is it wakes with a shout of delight,
And comes to our room with a smile that is
    bright?
Who is it springs into bed with a leap
And thinks it is queer that his dad wants to sleep?
Who answers his growling with laughter and tries
His patience by lifting the lids of his eyes?
Who jumps in the air and then lands with a thud
On his poor daddy's stomach? I'll tell you, it's
    Bud!

Who is it thinks life is but laughter and play
And doesn't know care is a part of the day?
Who is reckless of stockings and heedless of
    shoes?
Who laughs at a tumble and grins at a bruise?
Who climbs over fences and clambers up trees,
And scrapes all the skin off his shins and his
    knees?

Who sometimes comes home all bespattered with
   blood
That was drawn by a fall?   It's that rascal called
   Bud.

Yet, who is it makes all our toiling worth while?
Who can cure every ache that we know, by his
   smile?
Who is prince to his mother and king to his dad
And makes us forget that we ever were sad?
Who is center of all that we dream of and plan,
Our baby to-day but to-morrow our man?
It's that tough little, rough little tyke in the mud,
That tousled-haired, fun-loving rascal called Bud!

The Front Seat

When I was but a little lad I always liked to ride,
No matter what the rig we had, right by the
   driver's side.
The front seat was the honor place in bob-sleigh,
   coach or hack,
And I maneuvered to avoid the cushions in the
   back.
We children used to scramble then to share the
   driver's seat,
And long the pout I wore when I was not allowed
   that treat.

Though times have changed and I am old I still
confess I race
With other grown-ups now and then to get my
favorite place.

The auto with its cushions fine and big and easy
springs
Has altered in our daily lives innumerable things,
But hearts of men are still the same as what they
used to be,
When surreys were the stylish rigs, or so they
seem to me,
For every grown-up girl to-day and every grown-
up boy
Still hungers for the seat in front and scrambles
for its joy,
And riding by the driver's side still holds the
charm it did
In those glad, youthful days gone by when I was
just a kid.

I hurry, as I used to do, to claim that favorite
place,
And when a tonneau seat is mine I wear a solemn
face.
I try to hide the pout I feel, and do my best to
smile,

But envy of the man in front gnaws at me all
the while.

I want to be where I can see the road that lies
ahead,

To watch the trees go flying by and see the
country spread

Before me as we spin along, for there I miss the
fear

That seems to grip the soul of me while riding
in the rear.

And I am not alone in this. To-day I drive a car
And three glad youngsters madly strive to share
the "seat with Pa."

And older folks that ride with us, I very plainly
see,

Maneuver in their artful ways to sit in front with
me;

Though all the cushions in the world were piled
up in the rear,

The child in all of us still longs to watch the
engineer.

And happier hearts we seem to own when we're
allowed to ride,

No matter what the car may be, close by the
driver's side.

There Are No Gods

There are no gods that bring to youth
    The rich rewards that stalwarts claim;
The god of fortune is in truth
    A vision and an empty name.
The toiler who through doubt and care
    Unto his goal and victory plods,
With no one need his glory share:
    He is himself his favoring gods.

There are no gods that will bestow
    Earth's joys and blessings on a man.
Each one must choose the path he'll go,
    Then win from it what joy he can.
And he that battles with the odds
    Shall know success, but he who waits
The favors of the mystic gods,
    Shall never come to glory's gates.

No man is greater than his will;
    No gods to him will lend a hand!
Upon his courage and his skill
    The record of his life must stand.
What honors shall befall to him,
    What he shall claim of fame or pelf,
Depend not on the favoring whim
    Of fortune's god, but on himself.

The Auto

An auto is a helpful thing;
I love the way the motor hums,
I love each cushion and each spring,
The way it goes, the way it comes;
It saves me many a dreary mile,
It brings me quickly to the smile
Of those at home, and every day
It adds unto my time for play.

It keeps me with my friends in touch;
No journey now appears too much
To make with meetings at the end:
It gives me time to be a friend.
It laughs at distance, and has power
To lengthen every fleeting hour.
It bears me into country new
That otherwise I'd never view.

It's swift and sturdy and it strives
To fill with happiness our lives;
When for the doctor we've a need
It brings him to our door with speed.
It saves us hours of anxious care
And heavy heartache and despair.
It has its faults, but still I sing:
The auto is a helpful thing.

The Handy Man

The handy man about the house
Is old and bent and gray;
Each morning in the yard he toils,
Where all the children play;
Some new task every day he finds,
Some task he loves to do,
The handy man about the house,
Whose work is never through.

The children stand to see him toil,
And watch him mend a chair;
They bring their broken toys to him;
He keeps them in repair.
No idle moment Grandpa spends,
But finds some work to do,
And hums a snatch of some old song,
That in his youth he knew.

He builds with wood most wondrous things:
A table for the den,
A music rack to please the girls,
A gun case for the men.
And 'midst his paints and tools he smiles,
And seems as young and gay
As any of the little ones
Who round him run in play.

I stopped to speak with him awhile;
"Oh, tell me, Grandpa, pray,"
I said, "why do you work so hard
Throughout the livelong day?
Your hair is gray, your back is bent,
With weight of years oppressed;
This is the evening of your life—
Why don't you sit and rest?"

"Ah, no," the old man answered me,
"Although I'm old and gray,
I like to work out here where I
Can watch the children play.
The old have tasks that they must do;
The greatest of my joys
Is working on this shaded porch,
And mending children's toys."

And as I wandered on, I thought,
Oh, shall I lonely be
When time has powdered white my hair,
And left his mark on me?
Will little children round me play,
Shall I have work to do?
Or shall I be, when age is mine,
Lonely and useless too?

The New Days

The old days, the old days, how oft the poets
sing,
The days of hope at dewy morn, the days of
early spring,
The days when every mead was fair, and every
heart was true,
And every maiden wore a smile, and every sky
was blue;
The days when dreams were golden and every
night brought rest,
The old, old days of youth and love, the days
they say were best;
But I—I sing the new days, the days that lie
before,
The days of hope and fancy, the days that I
adore.

The new days, the new days, the selfsame days
they are;
The selfsame sunshine heralds them, the self-
same evening star
Shines out to light them on their way unto the
Bygone Land,
And with the selfsame arch of blue the world
to-day is spanned.
The new days, the new days, when friends are
just as true,

And maidens smile upon us all, the way they
used to do,
Dreams we know are golden dreams, hope springs
in every breast;
It cheers us in the dewy morn and soothes us
when we rest.

The new days, the new days, of them I want to
sing,
The new days with the fancies and the golden
dreams they bring;
The old days had their pleasures, but likewise
have the new
The gardens with their roses and the meadows
bright with dew;
We love to-day the selfsame way they loved in
days of old;
The world is bathed in beauty and it isn't growing
cold;
There's joy for us a-plenty, there are tasks for us
to do,
And life is worth the living, for the friends we
know are true.

The Call

Joy stands on the hilltops,
  Beckoning to me,
Urging me to journey
  Up where I can see
Blue skies ever smiling,
  Cool green fields below,
Hear the songs of children
  Still untouched by woe.

Joy stands on the hilltops,
  Urging me to stay,
Spite of toil and trouble,
  To life's rugged way,
Holding out a promise
  Of a life serene
When the steeps I've mastered
  Lying now between.

Joy stands on the hilltops,
  Smiling down at me,
Urging me to clamber
  Up where I can see
Over toil and trouble
  Far beyond despair,
And I answer smiling:
  Some day I'll be there.

Songs of Rejoicing

Songs of rejoicin',
  Of love and of cheer,
Are the songs that I'm yearnin' for
  Year after year.
The songs about children
  Who laugh in their glee
Are the songs worth the singin',
  The bright songs for me.

Songs of rejoicin',
  Of kisses and love,
Of faith in the Father,
  Who sends from above
The sunbeams to scatter
  The gloom and the fear;
These songs worth the singin',
  The songs of good cheer.

Songs of rejoicin',
  Oh, sing them again,
The brave songs of courage
  Appealing to men.
Of hope in the future
  Of heaven.the goal;
The songs of rejoicin'
  That strengthen the soul.

Another Mouth to Feed

We've got another mouth to feed,
  From out our little store;
To satisfy another's need
  Is now my daily chore.
A growing family is ours,
  Beyond the slightest doubt;
It takes all my financial powers
  To keep them looking stout.
With us another makes his bow
  To breakfast, dine and sup;
Our little circle's larger now,
  For Buddy's got a pup.

If I am frayed about the heels
  And both my elbows shine
And if my overcoat reveals
  The poverty that's mine,
'Tis not because I squander gold
  In folly's reckless way;
The cost of foodstuffs, be it told,
  Takes all my weekly pay.
'Tis putting food on empty plates
  That eats my wages up;
And now another mouth awaits,
  For Buddy's got a pup.

And yet I gladly stand the strain,
  And count the task worth while,

Nor will I dismally complain
　　While Buddy wears a smile.
What's one mouth more at any board
　　Though costly be the fare?
The poorest of us can afford
　　His frugal meal to share.
And so bring on the extra plate,
　　He will not need a cup,
And gladly will I pay the freight
　　Now Buddy's got a pup.

The Little Church

The little church of Long Ago, where as a boy
　　I sat
With mother in the family pew, and fumbled
　　with my hat—
How I would like to see it now the way I saw
　　it then,
The straight-backed pews, the pulpit high, the
　　women and the men
Dressed stiffly in their Sunday clothes and sol-
　　emnly devout,
Who closed their eyes when prayers were said
　　and never looked about—
That little church of Long Ago, it wasn't grand
　　to see,
But even as a little boy it meant a lot to me.

The choir loft where father sang comes back to
 me again;
I hear his tenor voice once more the way I
 heard it when
The deacons used to pass the plate, and once
 again I see
The people fumbling for their coins, as glad as
 they could be
To drop their quarters on the plate, and I'm a
 boy once more
With my two pennies in my fist that mother gave
 before
We left the house, and once again I'm reaching
 out to try
To drop them on the plate before the deacon
 passes by.

It seems to me I'm sitting in that high-backed
 pew, the while
The minister is preaching in that good old-
 fashioned style;
And though I couldn't understand it all some-
 how I know
The Bible was the text book in that church oi
 Long Ago;
He didn't preach on politics, but used the word
 of God,
And even now I seem to see the people gravely
 nod,

As though agreeing thoroughly with all he had
to say,
And then I see them thanking him before they
go away.

The little church of Long Ago was not a struc-
ture huge,
It had no hired singers or no other subterfuge
To get the people to attend, 'twas just a simple
place
Where every Sunday we were told about God's
saving grace;
No men of wealth were gathered there to help
it with a gift;
The only worldly thing it had—a mortgage hard
to lift.
And somehow, dreaming here to-day, I wish
that I could know
The joy of once more sitting in that church of
Long Ago.

Sue's Got a Baby

Sue's got a baby now, an' she
Is like her mother used to be;
Her face seems prettier, an' her ways
More settled-like. In these few days
She's changed completely, an' her smile
Has taken on the mother-style.
Her voice is sweeter, an' her words
Are clear as is the song of birds.
She still is Sue, but not the same—
She's different since the baby came.

There is a calm upon her face
That marks the change that's taken place;
It seems as though her eyes now see
The wonder things that are to be,
An' that her gentle hands now own
A gentleness before unknown.
Her laughter has a clearer ring
Than all thé bubbling of a spring,
An' in her cheeks love's tender flame
Glows brighter since the baby came.

I look at her an' I can see
Her mother as she used to be.
How sweet she was, an' yet how much
She sweetened by the magic touch

That made her mother! In her face
It seemed the angels left a trace
Of Heavenly beauty to remain
Where once had been the lines of pain
An' with the baby in her arms
Enriched her with a thousand charms.

Sue's got a baby now an' she
Is prettier than she used to be.
A wondrous change has taken place,
A softer beauty marks her face
An' in the warmth of her caress
There seems the touch of holiness,
An' all the charms her mother knew
Have blossomed once again in Sue.
I sit an' watch her an' I claim
My lost joys since her baby came.

The Lure That Failed

I know a wonderful land, I said,
    Where the skies are always blue,
Where on chocolate drops are the children fed,
    And cocoanut cookies, too;
Where puppy dogs romp at the children's feet,
    And the liveliest kittens play,
And little tin soldiers guard the street
    To frighten the bears away.

This land is reached by a wonderful ship
    That sails on a golden tide;
But never a grown-up makes the trip—
    It is only a children's ride.
And never a cross-patch journeys there,
    And never a pouting face,
For it is the Land of Smiling, where
    A frown is a big disgrace.

Oh, you board the ship when the sun goes down,
    And over a gentle sea
You slip away from the noisy town
    To the land of the chocolate tree.
And there, till the sun comes over the hill,
    You frolic and romp and play,
And of candy and cake you eat your fill,
    With no one to tell you "Nay!"

So come! It is time for the ship to go
　To this wonderful land so fair,
And gently the summer breezes blow
　To carry you safely there.
So come! Set sail on this golden sea,
　To the land that is free from dread!
"I know what you mean," she said to me,
"An' I don't wanna go to bed."

The Old-Fashioned Thanksgiving

It may be I am getting old and like too much to
　　dwell
Upon the days of bygone years, the days I loved
　　so well;
But thinking of them now I wish somehow that
　　I could know
A simple old Thanksgiving Day, like those of
　　long ago,
When all the family gathered round a table richly
　　spread,
With little Jamie at the foot and grandpa at the
　　head,
The youngest of us all to greet the oldest with a
　　smile,
With mother running in and out and laughing all
　　the while.

It may be I'm old-fashioned, but it seems to me
    to-day
We're too much bent on having fun to take the
    time to pray;
Each little family grows up with fashions of its
    own;
It lives within a world itself and wants to be
    alone.
It has its special pleasures, its circle, too, of
    friends;
There are no get-together days; each one his jour-
    ney wends,
Pursuing what he likes the best in his particular
    way,
Letting the others do the same upon Thanksgiving
    Day.

I like the olden way the best, when relatives were
    glad
To meet the way they used to do when I was but
    a lad;
The old home was a rendezvous for all our kith
    and kin,
And whether living far or near they all came
    trooping in
With shouts of "Hello, daddy!" as they fairly
    stormed the place

And made a rush for mother, who would stop to
    wipe her face
Upon her gingham apron before she kissed them
    all,
Hugging them proudly to her breast, the grown-
    ups and the small.

Then laughter rang throughout the home, and,
    Oh, the jokes they told;
From Boston, Frank brought new ones, but
    father sprang the old;
All afternoon we chatted, telling what we hoped
    to do,
The struggles we were making and the hardships
    we'd gone through;
We gathered round the fireside. How fast the
    hours would fly—
It seemed before we'd settled down 'twas time to
    say good-bye.
Those were the glad Thanksgivings, the old-time
    families knew
When relatives could still be friends and every
    heart was true.

The Old-Fashioned Pair

'Tis a little old house with a squeak in the stairs,
And a porch that seems made for just two easy
  chairs;
In the yard is a group of geraniums red,
And a glorious old-fashioned peony bed.
Petunias and pansies and larkspurs are there
Proclaiming their love for the old-fashioned pair.

Oh, it's hard now to picture the peace of the
  place!
Never lovelier smile lit a fair woman's face
Than the smile of the little old lady who sits
On the porch through the bright days of summer
  and knits.
And a courtlier manner no prince ever had
Than the little old man that she speaks of as
  "dad."

In that little old house there is nothing of hate;
There are old-fashioned things by an old-fash-
  ioned grate;
On the walls there are pictures of fine looking
  men
And beautiful ladies to look at, and then
Time has placed on the mantel to comfort them
  there
The pictures of grandchildren, radiantly fair.

Every part of the house seems to whisper of joy,
Save the trinkets that speak of a lost little boy.
Yet Time has long since soothed the hurt and
    the pain,
And his glorious memories only remain :
The laughter of children the old walls have
    known,
And the joy of it stays, though the babies have
    flown.

I am fond of that house and that old-fashioned
    pair
And the glorious calm that is hovering there.
The riches of life are not silver and gold
But fine sons and daughters when we are grown
    old,
And I pray when the years shall have silvered
    our hair
We shall know the delights of that old-fashioned
    pair.

At Pelletier's

We've been out to Pelletier's
Brushing off the stain of years,
Quitting all the moods of men
And been boys and girls again.
We have romped through orchards blazing,
Petted ponies gently grazing,
Hidden in the hayloft's spaces,
And the queerest sort of places
That are lost (and it's a pity!)
To the youngsters in the city.
And the hired men have let us
Drive their teams, and stopped to get us
Apples from the trees, and lingered
While a cow's cool nose we fingered;
And they told us all about her
And her grandpa who was stouter.

We've been out to Pelletier's
Watching horses raise their ears,
And their joyous whinnies hearing
When the man with oats was nearing.
We've been climbing trees an' fences
Never minding consequences.
And we helped the man to curry
The fat ponies' sides so furry.
And we saw a squirrel taking
Walnuts to the nest he's making,

Storing them for winter, when he
Can't get out to hunt for any.
And we watched the turkeys, growing
Big and fat and never knowing
That the reason they were living
Is to die for our Thanksgiving.

We've been out to Pelletier's,
Brushing off the stain of years.
We were kids set free from shamming
And the city's awful cramming,
And the clamor and the bustle
And the fearful rush and hustle—
Out of doors with room to race in
And broad acres soft to chase in.
We just stretched our souls and let them
Drop the petty cares that fret them,
Left our narrow thoughts behind us,
Loosed the selfish traits that bind us
And were wholesomer and plainer
Simpler, kinder folks and saner,
And at night said: "It's a pity
Mortals ever built a city."

At Christmas

A man is at his finest towards the finish of the
  year;
He is almost what he should be when the Christmas season's here;
Then he's thinking more of others than he's
  thought the months before,
And the laughter of his children is a joy worth
  toiling for.
He is less a selfish creature than at any other
  time;
When the Christmas spirit rules him he comes
  close to the sublime.

When it's Christmas man is bigger and is better
  in his part;
He is keener for the service that is prompted by
  the heart.
All the petty thoughts and narrow seem to vanish
  for awhile
And the true reward he's seeking is the glory of
  a smile.
Then for others he is toiling and somehow it
  seems to me
That at Christmas he is almost what God wanted
  him to be.

If I had to paint a picture of a man I think I'd
      wait
Till he'd fought his selfish battles and had put
      aside his hate.
I'd not catch him at his labors when his thoughts
      are all of pelf,
On the long days and the dreary when he's striv-
      ing for himself.
I'd not take him when he's sneering, when he's
      scornful or depressed,
But I'd look for him at Christmas when he's
      shining at his best.

Man is ever in a struggle and he's oft misunder-
      stood;
There are days the worst that's in him is the
      master of the good,
But at Christmas kindness rules him and he puts
      himself aside
And his petty hates are vanquished and his heart
      is opened wide.
Oh, I don't know how to say it, but somehow it
      seems to me
That at Christmas man is almost what God sent
      him here to be.

The Little Army

Little women, little men,
Childhood never comes again.
Live it gayly while you may;
Give your baby souls to play;
  March to sound of stick and pan,
    In your paper hats, and tramp
  Just as bravely as you can
    To your pleasant little camp.
Wooden sword and wooden gun
Make a battle splendid fun.
Fine the victories you win:
Dimpled cheek and dimpled chin.

Little women, little men,
Hearts are light when years are ten;
Eyes are bright and cheeks are red
When life's cares lie all ahead.
  Drums make merry music when
    They are leading children out;
  Trumpet calls are cheerful then,
    Glorious is the battle shout.
Little soldiers, single file,
Uniformed in grin and smile,
Conquer every foe they meet
Up and down the gentle street.

Little women, little men,
Would that youth could come again!
Would that I might fall in line
As a little boy of nine,
But with broomstick for a gun,
And with paper hat that I
Bravely wore back there for fun,
Never more may I defy
Foes that deep in ambush kneel—
Now my warfare's grim and real.
I that once was brave and bold,
Now am battered, bruised and old.

Little women, little men,
Planning to attack my den,
Little do you know the joy
That you give a worn-out boy
As he hears your gentle feet
Pitter-patting in the hall;
Gladly does he wait to meet
Conquest by a troop so small.
Dimpled cheek and dimpled chin,
You have but to smile to win.
Come and take him where he stays
Dreaming of his by-gone days.

Who Is Your Boss?

"I work for someone else," he said;
"I have no chance to get ahead.
At night I leave the job behind;
At morn I face the same old grind.
And everything I do by day
Just brings to me the same old pay.
While I am here I cannot see
The semblance of a chance for me."

I asked another how he viewed
The occupation he pursued.
"It's dull and dreary toil," said he,
"And brings but small reward to me.
My boss gets all the profits fine
That I believe are rightly mine.
My life's monotonously grim
Because I'm forced to work for him."

I stopped a third young man to ask
His attitude towards his task.
A cheerful smile lit up his face;
"I shan't be always in this place,"
He said, "because some distant day
A better job will come my way."
"Your boss?" I asked, and answered he:
"I'm going to make him notice me.

"He pays me wages and in turn
That money I am here to earn,
But I don't work for him alone;
Allegiance to myself I own.
I do not do my best because
It gets me favors or applause—
I work for him, but I can see
That actually I work for me.

"It looks like business good to me
The best clerk on the staff to be.
If customers approve my style
And like my manner and my smile
I help the firm to get the pelf,
But what is more I help myself.
From one big thought I'm never free:
That every day I work for me."

Oh, youth, thought I, you're bound to climb
The ladder of success in time.
Too many self-impose the cross
Of daily working for a boss,
Forgetting that in failing him
It is their own stars that they dim.
And when real service they refuse
They are the ones who really lose.

The Truth About Envy

I like to see the flowers grow,
To see the pansies in a row;
I think a well-kept garden's fine,
And wish that such a one were mine;
But one can't have a stock of flowers
Unless he digs and digs for hours.

My ground is always bleak and bare;
The roses do not flourish there.
And where I once sowed poppy seeds
Is now a tangled mass of weeds.
I'm fond of flowers, but admit,
For digging I don't care a bit.

I envy men whose yards are gay,
But never work as hard 'as they;
I also envy men who own
More wealth than I have ever known.
I'm like a lot of men who yearn
For joys that they refuse to earn.

You cannot have the joys of work
And take the comfort of a shirk.
I find the man I envy most
Is he who's longest at his post.
I could have gold and roses, too,
If I would work like those who do.

Living

If through the years we're not to do
   Much finer deeds than we have done;
If we must merely wander through
   Time's garden, idling in the sun;
If there is nothing big ahead,
Why do we fear to join the dead?

Unless to-morrow means that we
   Shall do some needed service here;
That tasks are waiting you and me
   That will be lost, save we appear;
Then why this dreadful thought of sorrow
That we may never see to-morrow?

If all our finest deeds are done,
   And all our splendor's in the past;
If there's no battle to be won,
   What matter if to-day's our last?
Is life so sweet that we would live
Though nothing back to life we give?

It is not greatness to have clung
   To life through eighty fruitless years;
The man who dies in action, young,
   Deserves our praises and our cheers,
Who ventures all for one great deed
And gives his life to serve life's need.

On Being Broke

Don't mind being broke at all,
    When I can say that what I had
Was spent for toys for kiddies small
    And that the spending made 'em glad.
I don't regret the money gone,
    If happiness it left behind.
An empty purse I'll look upon
    Contented, if its record's kind.
There's no disgrace in being broke,
    Unless it's due to flying high;
Though poverty is not a joke,
    The only thing that counts is "why?"

The dollars come to me and go;
    To-day I've eight or ten to spend;
To-morrow I'll be sailing low,
    And have to lean upon a friend.
But if that little bunch of mine
    Is richer by some toy or frill,
I'll face the world and never whine
    Because I lack a dollar bill.
I'm satisfied, if I can see
    One smile that hadn't bloomed before.
The only thing that counts with me
    Is what I've spent my money for.

I might regret my sorry plight,
    If selfishness brought it about;

If for the fun I had last night,
  Some joy they'd have to go without.
But if I've swapped my bit of gold,
  For laughter and a happier pack
Of youngsters in my little fold
  I'll never wish those dollars back.
If I have traded coin for things
  They needed and have left them glad,
Then being broke no sorrow brings—
  I've done my best with what I had.

The Broken Drum

There is sorrow in the household;
  There's a grief too hard to bear;
There's a little cheek that's tear-stained;
  There's a sobbing baby there.
And try how we will to comfort,
  Still the tiny teardrops come;
For, to solve a vexing problem,
  Curly Locks has wrecked his drum.

It had puzzled him and worried,
  How the drum created sound;
For he couldn't understand it;
  It was not enough to pound
With his tiny hands and drumsticks,
  And at last the day has come,

When another hope is shattered;
Now in ruins lies his drum.

With his metal bank he broke it,
Tore the tightened skin aside,
Gazed on vacant space bewildered,
Then he broke right down and cried.
For the broken bubble shocked him
And the baby tears must come;
Now a joy has gone forever:
Curly Locks has wrecked his drum.

While his mother tries to soothe him
I am sitting here alone;
In the life that lies behind me,
Many shocks like that I've known.
And the boy who's upstairs weeping,
In the years that are to come
Will learn that many pleasures
Are as empty as his drum.

Mother's Excuses

Mother for me made excuses
When I was a little tad;
Found some reason for my conduct
When it had been very bad.

Blamed it on a recent illness
Or my nervousness and told
Father to be easy with me
Every time he had to scold.

And I knew, as well as any
Roguish, healthy lad of ten,
Mother really wasn't telling
Truthful things to father then.
I knew I deserved the whipping,
Knew that I'd been very bad,
Knew that mother knew it also
When she intervened with dad.

I knew that my recent illness
Hadn't anything to do
With the mischief I'd been up to,
And I knew that mother knew.
But remembering my fever
And my nervous temperament,
Father put away the shingle
And postponed the sad event.

Now his mother, when I threaten
Punishment for this and that,
Calls to mind the dreary night hours
When beside his bed we sat.
Comes and tells me that he's nervous,
That's the reason he was bad,

And the boy and doting mother
Put it over on the dad.

Some day when he's grown as I am,
With a boy on mischief bent,
He will hear the timeworn story
Of the nervous temperament.
And remembering the shingle
That aside I always threw,
All I hope is that he'll let them
Put it over on him, too.

As It Is

I might wish the world were better,
    I might sit around and sigh
For a water that is wetter
    And a bluer sort of sky.
There are times I think the weather
    Could be much improved upon,
But when taken altogether
    It's a good old world we're on.
I might tell how I would make it,
    But when I have had my say
It is still my job to take it
    As it is, from day to day.

I might wish that men were kinder,
  And less eager after gold;
I might wish that they were blinder
  To the faults they now behold.
And I'd try to make them gentle,
  And more tolerant in strife
And a bit more sentimental
  O'er the finer things of life.
But I am not here to make them,
  Or to work in human clay;
It is just my work to take them
  As they are from day to day.

Here's a world that suffers sorrow,
  Here are bitterness and pain,
And the joy we plan to-morrow
  May be ruined by the rain.
Here are hate and greed and badness,
  Here are love and friendship, too,
But the most of it is gladness
  When at last we've run it through.
Could we only understand it
  As we shall some distant day,
We should see that He who planned it
  Knew our needs along the way.

A Boy's Tribute

Prettiest girl I've ever seen
    Is Ma.
Lovelier than any queen
    Is Ma.
Girls with curls go walking by,
Dainty, graceful, bold an' shy,
But the one that takes my eye
    Is Ma.

Every girl made into one
    Is Ma.
Sweetest girl to look upon
    Is Ma.
Seen 'em short and seen 'em tall,
Seen 'em big and seen 'em small,
But the finest one of all
    Is Ma.

Best of all the girls on earth
    Is Ma.
One that all the rest is worth
    Is Ma.
Some have beauty, some have grace,
Some look nice in silk and lace,
But the one that takes first place
    Is Ma.

Sweetest singer in the land
        Is Ma.
She that has the softest hand
        Is Ma.
Tenderest, gentlest nurse is she,
Full of fun as she can be,
An' the only girl for me
        Is Ma.

Bet if there's an angel here
        It's Ma.
If God has a sweetheart dear
        It's Ma.
Take the girls that artists draw,
An' all the girls I ever saw,
The only one without a flaw
        Is Ma.

Up to the Ceiling

Up to the ceiling
And down to the floor,
Hear him now squealing
And calling for more.
Laughing and shouting,
"Away up!" he cries.
Who could be doubting
The love in his eyes.
Heigho! my baby!
And heigho! my son!
Up to the ceiling
Is wonderful fun.

Bigger than daddy
And bigger than mother;
Only a laddie,
But bigger than brother.
Laughing and crowing
And squirming and wriggling,
Cheeks fairly glowing,
Now cooing and giggling!
Down to the cellar,
Then quick as a dart
Up to the ceiling
Brings joy to the heart.

Gone is the hurry,
The anguish and sting,

The heartache and worry
That business cares bring;
Gone is the hustle,
The clamor for gold,
The rush and the bustle
The day's affairs hold.
Peace comes to the battered
Old heart of his dad,
When "up to the ceiling"
He plays with his lad.

Thanksgiving

Gettin' together to smile an' rejoice,
An' eatin' an' laughin' with folks of your choice;
An' kissin' the girls an' declarin' that they
Are growin' more beautiful day after day;
Chattin' an' braggin' a bit with the men,
Buildin' the old family circle again;
Livin' the wholesome an' old-fashioned cheer,
Just for awhile at the end of the year.

Greetings fly fast as we crowd through the door
And under the old roof we gather once more
Just as we did when the youngsters were small;
Mother's a little bit grayer, that's all.
Father's a little bit older, but still
Ready·to romp an' to laugh with a will.

Here we are back at the table again
Tellin' our stories as women an' men.

Bowed are our heads for a moment in prayer;
Oh, but we're grateful an' glad to be there.
Home from the east land an' home from the west,
Home with the folks that are dearest an' best.
Out of the sham of the cities afar
We've come for a time to be just what we are.
Here we can talk of ourselves an' be frank,
Forgettin' position an' station an' rank.

Give me the end of the year an' its fun
When most of the plannin' an' toilin' is done;
Bring all the wanderers home to the nest,
Let me sit down with the ones I love best,
Hear the old voices still ringin' with song,
See the old faces unblemished by wrong,
See the old table with all of its chairs
An' I'll put soul in my Thanksgivin' prayers.

The Boy Soldier

Each evening on my lap there climbs
    A little boy of three,
·And with his dimpled, chubby fists
    He pounds me shamefully.
He gives my beard a vicious tug,
    He bravely pulls my nose;

And then he tussles with my hair
And then explores my clothes.

He throws my pencils on the floor;
My watch is his delight;
He never seems to think that I
Have any private right.
And though he breaks my good cigars,
With all his cunning art,
He works a greater ruin, far,
Deep down within my heart.

This roguish little tyke who sits
Each night upon my knee,
And hammers at his poor old dad,
Is bound to conquer me.
He little knows that long ago,
He forced the gates apart,
And marched triumphantly into
The city of my heart.

Some day perhaps, in years to come,
When he is older grown,
He, too, will be assailed as I,
By youngsters of his own.
And when at last a little lad
Gives battle on his knee,
I know that he'll be captured, too,
Just as he captured me.

My Land

My land is where the kind folks are,
  And where the friends are true,
Where comrades brave will travel far
  Some kindly deed to do.
My land is where the smiles are bright
  And where the speech is sweet,
And where men cling to what is right
  Regardless of defeat.

My land is where the starry flag
  Gleams brightly in the sun;
The land of rugged mountain crag,
  The land where rivers run,
Where cheeks are tanned and hearts are bold
  And women fair to see,
And all is not a strife for gold—
  That land is home to me.

My land is where the children play,
  And where the roses bloom,
And where to break the peaceful day
  No flaming cannons boom.
My land's the land of honest toil,
  Of laughter, dance and song,
Where harvests crown the fertile soil
  And thoughtful are the strong.

My land's the land of many creeds
  And tolerance for all;
It is the land of splendid deeds
  Where men are seldom small.
And though the world should bid me roam,
  Its distant scenes to see,
My land would keep my heart at home
  And there I'd always be.

Daddies

I would rather be the daddy
  Of a romping, roguish crew,
Of a bright-eyed chubby laddie
  And a little girl or two,
Than the monarch of a nation
  In his high and lofty seat
Taking empty adoration
  From the subjects at his feet.

I would rather own their kisses
  As at night to me they run,
Than to be the king who misses
  All the simpler forms of fun.
When his dreary day is ending
  He is dismally alone,

But when my sun is descending
   There are joys for me to own.

He may ride to horns and drumming;
   I must walk a quiet street,
But when once they see me coming
   Then on joyous, flying feet
They come racing to me madly
   And I catch them with a swing
And I say it proudly, gladly,
   That I'm happier than a king.

You may talk of lofty places,
   You may boast of pomp and power,
Men may turn their eager faces
   To the glory of an hour,
But give me the humble station
   With its joys that long survive,
For the daddies of the nation
   Are the happiest men alive.

Loafing

Under the shade of trees,
Flat on my back at ease,
Lulled by the hum of bees,
   There's where I rest;
Breathing the scented air,

Lazily loafing there,
Never a thought of care,
  Peace in my breast.

There where the waters run,
Laughing along in fun,
I go when work is done,
  There's where I stray;
Couch of a downy green,
Restful and sweet and clean,
Set in a fairy scene,
  Wondrously gay.

Worn out with toil and strife,
Sick of the din of life,
With pain and sorrow rife,
  There's where I go;
Soothing and sweet I find,
Comforts that ease the mind,
Leaving dull care behind,
  Rest there I know.

Flat on my back I lie,
Watching the ships go by,
Under the fleecy sky,
  Day dreaming there;
From grief I find surcease,
From worry gain release,
Resting in perfect peace,
  Free from all care.

When Father Played Baseball

The smell of arnica is strong,
  And mother's time is spent
In rubbing father's arms and back
  With burning liniment.
The house is like a druggist's shop;
  Strong odors fill the hall,
And day and night we hear him groan,
  Since father played baseball.

He's forty past, but he declared
  That he was young as ever;
And in his youth, he said, he was
  A baseball player clever.
So when the business men arranged
  A game, they came to call
On dad and asked him if he thought
  That he could play baseball.

"I haven't played in fifteen years,"
  Said father, "but I know
That I can stop the grounders hot,
  And I can make the throw.
I used to play a corking game;
  The curves, I know them all;
And you can count on me, you bet,
  To join your game of ball."

On Saturday the game was played,
　　And all of us were there;
Dad borrowed an old uniform,
　　That Casey used to wear.
He paid three dollars for a glove,
　　Wore spikes to save a fall;
He had the make-up on all right,
　　When father played baseball.

At second base they stationed him;
　　A liner came his way;
Dad tried to stop it with his knee,
　　And missed a double play.
He threw into the bleachers twice,
　　He let a pop fly fall;
Oh, we were all ashamed of him,
　　When father played baseball.

He tried to run, but tripped and fell,
　　He tried to take a throw;
It put three fingers out of joint,
　　And father let it go.
He stopped a grounder with his face;
　　Was spiked, nor was that all;
It looked to us like suicide,
　　When father played baseball.

At last he limped away, and now
　　He suffers in disgrace;

His arms are bathed in liniment;
   Court plaster hides his face.
He says his back is breaking, and
   His legs won't move at all;
It made a wreck of father when
   He tried to play baseball.

The smell of arnica abounds;
   He hobbles with a cane;
A row of blisters mar his hands;
   He is in constant pain.
But lame and weak as father is,
   He swears he'll lick us all
If we dare even speak about
   The day he played baseball.

About Boys

Show me the boy who never threw
   A stone at someone's cat;
Or never hurled a snowball swift
   At someone's high silk hat.
Who never ran away from school,
   To seek the swimming hole;
Or slyly from a neighbor's yard
   Green apples never stole.

Show me the boy who never broke
    A pane of window glass;
Who never disobeyed the sign
    That says: "Keep off the grass."
Who never did a thousand things,
    That grieve us sore to tell;
And I'll show you a little boy
    Who must be far from well.

Curly Locks

Curly locks, what do you know of the world,
    And what do your brown eyes see?
Has your baby mind been able to find
    One thread of the mystery?
Do you know of the sorrow and pain that lie
    In the realms that you've never seen?
Have you even guessed of the great unrest
    In the world where you've never been?

Curly locks, what do you know of the world
    And what do you see in the skies?
When you solemnly stare at the world out there
    Can you see where the future lies?
What wonderful thoughts are you thinking now?
    Can it be that you really know
That beyond your youth there are joy and ruth,
    On the way that you soon must go?

Baby's Got a Tooth

The telephone rang in my office to-day, as it
    often has tinkled before.
I turned in my chair in a half-grouchy way, for
    a telephone call is a bore;
And I thought, "It is somebody wanting to know
    the distance from here to Pekin."
In a tone that was gruff I shouted "Hello," a
    sign for the talk to begin.
"What is it?" I asked in a terrible way. I was
    huffy, to tell you the truth,
Then over the wire I heard my wife say: "The
    baby, my dear, has a tooth!"

I have seen a man jump when the horse that he
    backed finished first in a well-driven race.
I have heard the man cheer, as a matter of fact,
    and I've seen the blood rush to his face;
I've been on the spot when good news has come
    in and I've witnessed expressions of glee
That range from a yell to a tilt of the chin; and
    some things have happened to me
That have thrilled me with joy from my toes to
    my head, but never from earliest youth
Have I jumped with delight as I did when she
    said, "The baby, my dear, has a tooth."

I have answered the telephone thousands of times
    for messages both good and bad;

I've received the reports of most horrible crimes,
    and news that was cheerful or sad;
I've been telephoned this and been telephoned
    that, a joke, or an errand to run;
I've been called to the phone for the idlest of chat,
    when there was much work to be done;
But never before have I realized quite the thrill
    of a message, forsooth,
Till over the wire came these words that I write,
    "The baby, my dear, has a tooth."

Home and the Baby

Home was never home before,
    Till the baby came.
Love no golden jewels wore,
    Till the baby came.
There was joy, but now it seems
Dreams were not the rosy dreams,
Sunbeams not such golden beams—
    Till the baby came.

Home was never really gay,
    Till the baby came.
I'd forgotten how to play,
    Till the baby came.

Smiles were never half so bright,
Troubles never half so light,
Worry never took to flight,
  Till the baby came.

Home was never half so blest,
  Till the baby came.
Lacking something that was best,
  Till the baby came.
Kisses were not half so sweet,
Love not really so complete,
Joy had never found our street
  Till the baby came.

The Fisherman

Along a stream that raced and ran
  Through tangled trees and over stones,
That long had heard the pipes o' Pan
  And shared the joys that nature owns,
I met a fellow fisherman,
  Who greeted me in cheerful tones.

The lines of care were on his face.
  I guessed that he had buried dead;
Had run for gold full many a race,
  And kept great problems in his head,

But in that gentle resting place
   No word of wealth or fame he said.

He showed me trout that he had caught
   And praised the larger ones of mine;
Told me how that big beauty fought
   And almost broke his silken line;
Spoke of the trees and sky, and thought
   Them proof of life and power divine.

There man to man we talked of trees
   And birds, as people talk of men;
Discussed the busy ways of bees;
   Wondered what lies beyond our ken;
Where is the land no mortal sees,
   And shall we come this way again.

"Out here," he told me, with a smile,
   "Away from all the city's sham,
The strife for splendor and for style,
   The ticker and the telegram
I come for just a little while
   To be exactly as I am."

Foes think the bad in him they've guessed
   And prate about the wrong they scan;
Friends that have seen him at his best
   Believe they know his every plan;
I know him better than the rest,
   I know him as a fisherman.

The March of Mortality

Over the hills of time to the valley of endless
    years;
Over the roads of woe to the land that is free
    from tears;
Up from the haunts of men to the place where the
    angels are,
This is the march of mortality to a wonderful
    goal afar.

Troopers we are in life, warring at times with
    wrong,
But promised ever unbroken rest at last in a land
    of song;
And whether we serve or rule, and whether we
    fall or rise,
We shall come, in time, to that golden vale where
    never the spirit dies.

Back of the strife for gain, and under the toil
    for fame,
The dreams of men in this mortal march have
    ever remained the same.
They have lived through their days and years for
    the great rewards to be,
When earth's dusty garb shall be laid aside for
    the robes of eternity.

This is the march of mortality, whatever man's
    race or creed,
And whether he's one of the savage tribe or one
    of a higher breed,
He is conscious dimly of better things that were
    promised him long ago,
And he keeps his place in the line with men for
    the joys that his soul shall know.

Growing Down

Time was I thought of growing up,
    But that was ere the babies came;
I'd dream and plan to be a man
    And win my share of wealth and fame,
For age held all the splendors then
    And wisdom seemed life's brightest crown
For mortal brow. It's different now.
    Each evening finds me growing down.

I'm not so keen for growing up
    To wrinkled cheek and heavy tongue,
And sluggish blood; with little Bud
    I long to be a comrade young.
His sports are joys I want to share,
    His games are games I want to play,
An old man grim's no chum for him
    And so I'm growing down to-day.

I'm back to marbles and to tops,
    To flying kites and one-ol'-cat;
"Fan acres!" I now loudly cry;
    I also take my turn at bat;
I've had my fling at growing up
    And want no old man's fair renown.
To be a boy is finer joy,
    And so I've started growing down.

Once more I'm learning games I knew
    When I was four and five and six,
I'm going back along life's track
    To find the same old-fashioned tricks,
And happy are the hours we spend
    Together, without sigh or frown.
To be a boy is Age's joy,
    And so to him I'm growing down.

The Roads of Happiness

The roads of happiness are not
    The selfish roads of pleasure seeking,
Where cheeks are flushed with haste and hot
    And none has time for kindly speaking.
But they're the roads where lovers stray,
    Where wives and husbands walk together
And children romp along the way
    Whenever it is pleasant weather.

When Mother Sleeps

When mother sleeps, a slamming door
   Disturbs her not at all;
A man might walk across the floor
   Or wander through the hall;
A pistol shot outside would not
   Drive slumber from her eyes—
But she is always on the spot
   The moment baby cries.

The thunder crash she would not hear,
   Nor shouting in the street;
A barking dog, however near,
   Of sleep can never cheat
Dear mother, but I've noticed this
   To my profound surprise:
That always wide-awake she is
   The moment baby cries.

However weary she may be,
   Though wrapped in slumber deep,
Somehow it always seems to me
   Her vigil she will keep.
Sound sleeper that she is, I take
   It in her heart there lies
A love that causes her to wake
   The moment baby cries.

The Weaver

The patter of rain on the roof,
  The glint of the sun on the rose;
Of life, these the warp and the woof,
  The weaving that everyone knows.
Now grief with its consequent tear,
  Now joy with its luminous smile;
The days are the threads of the year—
  Is what I am weaving worth while?

What pattern have I on my loom?
  Shall my bit of tapestry please?
Am I working with gray threads of gloom?
  Is there faith in the figures I seize?
When my fingers are lifeless and cold,
  And the threads I no longer can weave
Shall there be there for men to behold
  One sign of the things I believe?

God sends me the gray days and rare,
  The threads from his bountiful skein,
And many, as sunshine, are fair.
  And some are as dark as the rain.
And I think as I toil to express
  My life through the days slipping by,
Shall my tapestry prove a success?
  What sort of a weaver am I?

Am I making the most of the red
   And the bright strands of luminous gold?
Or blotting them out with the thread
   By which all men's failure is told?
Am I picturing life as despair,
   As a thing men shall shudder to see,
Or weaving a bit that is fair
   That shall stand as the record of me?

The Few

The easy roads are crowded
   And the level roads are jammed;
The pleasant little rivers
   With the drifting folks are crammed.
But off yonder where it's rocky,
   Where you get a better view,
You will find the ranks are thinning
   And the travelers are few.

Where the going's smooth and pleasant
   You will always find the throng,
For the many, more's the pity,
   Seem to like to drift along.
But the steeps that call for courage,
   And the task that's hard to do
In the end result in glory
   For the never-wavering few.

Real Swimming

I saw him in the distance, as the train went
    speeding by,
A shivery little fellow standing in the sun to dry.
And a little pile of clothing very near him I could
    see:
He was owner of a gladness that had once
    belonged to me.
I have shivered as he shivered, I have dried the
    way he dried,
I've stood naked in God's sunshine with my gar-
    ments at my side;
And I thought as I beheld him, of the many
    weary men
Who would like to go in swimming as a little
    boy again.

I saw him scarce a moment, yet I knew his lips
    were blue
And I knew his teeth were chattering just as mine
    were wont to do;
And I knew his merry playmates in the pond were
    splashing still;
I could tell how much he envied all the boys that
    never chill;
And throughout that lonesome journey, I kept
    living o'er and o'er
The joys of going swimming when no bathing
    suits we wore;

I was with that little fellow, standing chattering
    in the sun;
I was sharing in his shivers and a partner of his
    fun.

Back to me there came the pictures that I never
    shall forget
When I dared not travel homewards if my shock
    of hair was wet,
When I did my brief undressing under fine and
    friendly trees
In the days before convention rigged us up in
    b. v. d's.
And I dived for stones and metal on the mill
    pond's muddy floor,
Then stood naked in the sunshine till my blood
    grew warm once more.
I was back again, a youngster, in those golden
    days of old,
When my teeth were wont to chatter and my lips
    were blue with cold.

The Love of the Game

There is too much of sighing, and weaving
  Of pitiful tales of despair.
There is too much of wailing and grieving,
  And too much of railing at care.
There is far too much glorification
  Of money and pleasure and fame;
But I sing the joy of my station,
  And I sing the love of my game.

There is too much of tremble-lip telling
  Of hurts that have come with the fight.
There is too much of pitiful dwelling
  On plans that have failed to go right.
There is too much of envious pining
  For luxuries others may claim.
Too much thought of wining and dining,
  But I sing the love of my game.

There is too much of grim magnifying
  The troubles that come with the day,
There is too much indifferent trying
  To travel a care-beset way.
Too much do men think of gold-getting,
  Too much have they underwrit shame,
Which accounts for the frowning and fretting,
  But I sing the joy of my game.

INDEX OF FIRST LINES

4 - 3/08

4 3/05
4 - 3/05